THE
DOGS OF WAR SERIES
VOLUME 7

BLOOD AND ICE

by

Leo Kessler

KT-163-703

SPELLMOUNT

British Library Cataloguing in Publication Data:
A catalogue record for this book is available
from the British Library

Copyright © Charles Whiting 2006

ISBN 1-86227-334-0

First published in the UK in 1977.
Reprinted in 2006 by
Spellmount Limited
The Mill
Brimscombe Port
Stroud
Gloucestershire
GL5 2QG
UK

Tel: 0044 (0) 1453 883300
Fax: 0044 (0) 1453 883233
E-mail: enquiries@spellmount.com
Website: www.spellmount.com

1 3 5 7 9 8 6 4 2

The right of Charles Whiting to be identified
as the author of this work has been asserted by him
in accordance with the Copyright, Designs
and Patents Act 1988

Printed in Great Britain by
Oaklands Book Services
Stonehouse, Gloucestershire GL10 3RQ

THE LAST BATTLE!

'And he is dead who will not fight,
and who dies fighting has increase.'
Julian Grenfell, 'Into Battle' *1916*

'Rather dead than Red.'
Popular German Saying, 1945

'Oh, left-wing thinkers and intellectuals,
students of the avant-garde. When you hear
the barked command "Hands behind your backs"
and begin the march towards the archipelago,
only then will you begin to understand.'
Solzhenitsyn, 'Gulag Archipelago' *1973*

SECTION ONE:

SS REGIMENT EUROPA

ONE

'*Cavalry!*'

Sergeant-Major Schulze, in charge of the little convoy of SS men, the survivors of SS Regiment Wotan, did not open his eyes.

The Corporal licked his lips anxiously and looked again at the dark shapes on horseback moving across the snow-capped height, parallel with the Hungarian road. 'Schulze,' he shook the big NCO's shoulder, 'there's somebody up there, watching us! Looks like the Ivans to me.'

'Christ!' Schulze groaned. 'Can't even sleep in this bloody army!' He sat up and stared at the black flecks about half a kilometre away. They had to be Russians. The 4th SS Panzer Corps which was defending this part of the Hungarian front was desperately short of men: that is why they, the pathetic handful of survivors from the ill-fated Ardennes Offensive, were being rushed to the East.

Schulze glanced at the two halftracks rattling along behind him at regulation convoy distance, their decks covered with camouflage nets against air attack. Below them the exhausted SS men, who had been travelling three days now, would be asleep like the men snoring all around him. 'What do you think?' the Corporal, who was the airlookout, asked anxiously.

'Shut up!' Schulze said brutally. 'I'm thinking where the Ivans are going to hit us.' Schulze made up his mind. He stood up and whistled shrilly. The driver of the second halftrack heard the whistle. His head spun in Schulze's direction.

Carefully, Schulze placed his hand on the top of his helmet,
fingers outstretched. It was the infantry signal for 'rally on me'.
The driver understood at once. He accelerated. Behind him the
other driver did the same. Schulze crawled over the sleeping men,
kicking each one in turn and shouting: 'Don't grow corns on yer
asses! ...Move yourselves!'

Everywhere the exhausted men began to sit up, grumbling
and cursing and reaching automatically for their weapons. They
were veterans. They knew Schulze would only wake them if
there were trouble.

Schulze balanced himself precariously on the swaying back of
the halftrack. The second vehicle was about a metre and a half
behind but he dare not stop the convoy to transmit his orders,
just in case there were other Russians waiting for them in the
firs on either side of the little road. He took a deep breath and
launched himself into the air.

His big feet crashed onto the halftrack's blunt snout. His hands
clutched desperately and next instant he was dragging himself
over the metal windshield into the cab. He banged the butt of his
Schmeisser machine pistol hard against the metal side of the cab.
'Shake those little sleepy heads of yours awake,' he yelled, 'while
you've still got some to shake.'

The worn, unshaven men of the second halftrack came to
life.

'Now listen,' Schulze said. 'We've got visitors up there,' he
jerked a big dirty thumb at the skyline, 'Popovs! Right, stand by
the lot of you and when they hit us – which they will – I want
you lot to show off like ten naked niggers. Remember you lot
are *Wotan.*'

They grinned back. Nothing ever seemed to shake *SS
Hauptscharführer* Schulze!

The village was typically Hungarian – a collection of shabby
white-painted cottages with straw roofs, now heavy with snow
surrounded by little tumbledown picket fences. But there was

something strange about this one. No smoke was coming from the cottages, yet a herd of sheep, shivering and trembling in the cold, stood grouped by the roadside. Schulze glanced at the skyline. The cavalry had disappeared.

He acted at once. 'All right,' he bellowed above the clatter of the halftracks, 'I think this is where the Ivans have decided to welcome us to the Eastern Front!'

The SS troopers in their camouflaged, green mottled overalls needed no urging. Hurriedly they positioned themselves behind the vehicle's metal sides, weapons at the ready. Schulze nodded at the driver. He put his foot down on the accelerator and the halftrack shot forward, throwing up clouds of snow on both sides like the wake of a fast ship.

Schulze fired a burst over the driver's head. The sheep, jostling and bumping into each other crazily, fled down the road into the daisy chain of mines which had been spread across it in anticipation of this moment. The first mine exploded with a thick impressive crump. Angry scarlet flame shot upwards, sending animals hurtling through the air. The halftracks sped along the smoking road, and started to take the first wild bursts of enemy slugs on their armour.

The Russians were everywhere but the ease with which the SS carriers had passed the little mine barrier surprised them. Their fire was wild and erratic. Schulze gave them no chance to recover. With his men firing from behind the cover of their vehicles, the enemy bullets whining off them harmlessly, he led them through the ambush at a hellish speed. A satchel charge hurtled through the air. The driver swerved just in time. It exploded in the middle of the road, sending the ten ton carrier swaying back and forth like a ship at sea. Schulze poured an angry burst of nine mm slugs into the cottage from which the grenades had been thrown. A man fell out of the window, his face gone, hands fanning the air crazily.

They were nearly out now. Schulze glanced behind him. The other two halftracks had made it too, both their windscreens cracked into glass spiderwebs. He breathed a sigh of relief. 'We're nearly out of this shit –' he began.

He never finished his sentence. It was then that the Russian cavalry hit them, streaming out of a side track between the last of the cottages, knouts lashing the sweat-lathered bodies of their horses, curved swords whirling in silver flashes, strange cries torn from their gaping mouths.

'*Kusacken*'[1] someone yelled in fear.

Schulze knew why. The Cossacks took prisoners, but only for long enough to plunder them of their possessions and practice primitive barbarities on them before finishing them off. 'All right, keep cool. They've not got as far as sawing off yer balls with those penknives yet.'

Swiftly he switched the machine pistol to single shots and fired at the first rider with the silver insignia of a Cossack captain. The man flew over the streaming mane of his black horse, the silver curve of his sword sailing high into the air.

The rest of the troopers in the halftrack followed his example and the morning air was full of yells, curses, screams, cries of agony. But still they came on. The first of the Cossacks drew parallel with the halftracks. Schulze flicked to automatic and fired a wild burst. The leading Cossack's horse was hit. Red flowers of blood erupted suddenly the whole length of it flank. The stallion reared high into the air, its hooves flailing wildly in an ecstasy of agony.

Just as the stallion went down, the rider launched himself into the air. His dirty paws sought and found a grip on the halftrack and with a grunt he hauled himself over the side and on to the deck. His knife flashed in the weak yellow winter sun, and then plunged deep into the driver's back. Schulze reacted in a flash and crashed the butt of his Schmeisser, cruelly into the back of the Cossack's skull, crushing it like a soft-boiled egg. A moment

1. Cossacks.

later the halftrack slammed hard against a great oak to the left of the road and came to an abrupt halt.

Behind them, the two other halftracks were forced to brake, skidding wildly on the slick snow surface, as their drivers tried desperately to avoid crashing into the lead vehicle, sprawled crazily halfway across the road.

'*Urrah!*' a great cry burst from the Cossacks' throats as they urged their horses forward their manes streaming wildly behind them.

The leaders did not even rein in as they came level, but dropped straight from the saddles on to the halftracks. Instantly the decks of the German vehicles were transformed into a wild, cursing, swaying mass of men, fighting for naked survival.

A huge bearded Cossack, his broad dark face pitted with pockmarks, grabbed for Schulze's testicles in the middle of the *mêlée*. Schulze did not give him a chance. He crashed his elbow into the man's mouth. The Cossack went back, spitting out broken yellow teeth. Tumbling backwards, Schulze smashed the steel-plated heel of his jackboot into the Cossack's face, crying, 'Try my dice-beaker on for size, Popov!'

Arms suddenly grabbed him around his neck. He squirmed his head round. A handsome young boy was glaring down at him, his dark eyes gleaming with hate and determination. Schulze thrust his two fingers upwards. They lodged inside the boy's nostrils. Schulze crooked them and tugged hard in one swift movement. The Cossack screamed hysterically in sheer, absolute agony. Hot blood streamed down Schulze's wrist as the boy's nose burst and he fainted across Schulze's body.

The morning air was suddenly heavy with the rattle of tank tracks and the tremendous crack of an 88mm cannon. The shell passed over their heads and crashed in the village beyond. All at once the Cossacks were running for their lives as the first Royal Tiger, all seventy-two tons of it, came to a halt next to the leading halftrack and began sawing the air with its twin machine guns.

'Holy shit!' Schulze breathed out hard and wiped the sweat from his dripping brow with a hand that trembled visibly. 'I thought they'd sabred my balls off that time...'

TWO

Their rescuers kicked and shoved the Cossack prisoners on to their knees in the snow in a long line, their backs to the Royal Tigers. A tall emaciated officer in the uniform of an *Obersturmbannführer* limped towards the first of the prisoners, pistol already in hand. The left eye of his skinny, hawklike face was covered with a patch and his left sleeve was empty, tucked into the side of his gleaming black belt. From the way he limped, Schulze guessed most of his left leg was missing too.

Carefully the *Obersturmbannführer* placed the muzzle of his pistol behind the right ear of the first prisoner. The Cossack tensed expectantly, but did not cry out. The officer's face tightened. He pressed the trigger. The pistol jerked upwards and the back of the prisoner's head disappeared in a sudden gush of bright red blood.

The officer's face was expressionless. Turning for a moment, he cried to the awestricken young soldiers with the *Europa* armband: 'Another Russian pig less!'

He stepped over the body and placing his pistol against the base of the next man's skull, pressed the trigger.

'Who the hell is he?' Schulze asked the two young troopers of the rescue force standing next to him.

'*Niet verstan*,' the one said. '*Comprends pas*,' said the other. Schulze groaned to himself, knowing instinctively that he had landed himself in yet another hole.

15

'Who is the senior non-commissioned officer?' rasped the hawkface *Obersturmbannführer*. Behind him two of his men were draping the black and white *Europa* armbands across each of the dead Cossacks – 'so the pigs will know who did it when they come to collect their carrion.'

'Sergeant-major Schulze, *Obersturmbannführer*! he bellowed, knowing that he could not pull any of his old *Wotan* stuff with this man.

'Report, Sarnt-Major?'

'Report respectfully, survivors of *SS Panzer Regiment Wotan*, thirty effectives, eighteen wounded, *Obersturmbannführer*!'

The skinny officer took in Schulze's impressive bulk – the Silver Wound Medal, Tank-Assault Badge in Gilt, the German Cross in Gold, the Knight's Cross of the Iron Cross at his throat – and seemed pleased with what he saw.

'My name is Habicht,' the officer said. 'I welcome you and your men to *Viking*¹ and, in particular, to *SS Regiment Europa*. We have need of experienced men like yours, especially NCOs.'

Schulze ventured a question. 'But are your men German, sir?'

'Only a few of them – and they are Ethnic Germans. The rest are from half a dozen European countries. All volunteers, fighting for the cause of Europe against the Red plague. His solitary eye gleamed with sudden fanaticism. 'And we shall triumph. Final victory will still be ours, come what may… All right, tell your men to mount. We must get out of this damned partisan country before the Bolshevik swine return.'

Schulze stood in silent amazement. Were there still officers, even in the Armed SS who believed in final victory? Everybody knew that Germany was beaten. The sparrows were singing it off the roofs, if there were any roofs left, that was. Slowly Sergeant-

---

1. The 5th *SS Panzer Division*, to which the *Europa* belonged.

Major Schulze stamped across the scuffed, blood-stained snow, telling himself glumly that the survivors of *Wotan* were in the shit again, right up to their necks in it.

As the three halftracks, led by the troop of Royal Tigers, swung into the main street of the little Hungarian town of Komarom, Schulze could see that his guess was correct. On both sides of the main street there were piles of ammunition boxes and jer-ricans full of petrol, ready for immediate use. In an alley there was a line of armoured halftracks, their sides painted with a big red cross. *Hiwis*[2] mostly yellow-faced, slant-eyed Turcomen and Siberians, were everywhere, stacking fresh crates of food. It was clear that a new offensive was about to begin and *Europa* would undoubtedly be part of it.

Schulze, satisfied everything was under control, walked wearily to the tumbledown wooden hut that the guide had said was his, and thrust open the door, ready to fling himself on his bunk and sleep.

But the hut was already occupied. A yellow-faced *Hiwi* was sitting there, a bland smile on his lips, a thin black moustache reaching down below his double chin, happily running a lighted match along the seam of his shirt to kill the lice.

'What the hell is this?' Schulze bellowed. 'Am I in a Jewish whorehouse or something?'

The *Hiwi* smiled happily at him and blew out his match. 'You want whorehouse, Sergeant-Major? Not Yiddie. But Hungarian girls make fucki-fucki very good.' He made his meaning quite clear with an obscene gesture of his thumb and fingers. The Hiwi got to his feet and began putting on his tunic. 'I Chink. All German soldiers call me Chink. I driver – your servant, Sergeant-Major.'

---

2. Former Russian POWs in German hands who had volunteered for auxiliary service in the German Army. By 1945 there were 600,000 of them.

He completed putting on his tunic and Schulze gasped. It bore the *Europa* armnband. He moaned and clapped a hand to his forehead. 'A bloody Chink in SS uniform; What would the Führer say!' Schulze slumped into the only available chair. 'All right, you slant-eyed Siberian shit. There's a tin of fifty cigarettes in my pack. Take it. Get me a woman, a bottle of firewater and a packet of Parisians[3] extra strong. I hear all these Hungarian whores are poxed-up to the eyes. And then trot back here with them – double-time.'

'Chink, he back in double time,' he cried and went out, clutching the tin to his fat chest, as if it were the Holy Grail itself.

'Oh, my aching back!' Schulze gasped in wonder as Chink proudly escorted the whore through the door, a bottle of schnaps in one hand. The red-haired Hungarian girl seemed to have been sewn into her short, tight skirt. It revealed the soft rounded curve of her buttocks and her crotch, as if she were naked. Her frilly embroidered peasant blouse was little better. She had pulled it so tight that her large, well-nippled breasts seemed about to burst through the semi-transparent material. Schulze rose to his feet, big paws stretched out eagerly. The girl giggled hysterically, revealing a mouthful of gold teeth, as Schulze hands sought and found her breasts, which were as big and as firm as fresh melons.

The Chink beamed his approval and put the bottle on the rickety wooden bed. 'Watch bed, Sergeant-Major. He not much good for fucki-fucki.'

But Sergeant-Major Schulze was not fated to enjoy the Hungarian whore's ample charms that particular afternoon. Abruptly a shadow darkened the entrance to the little hut and *Obersturmbannführer* Habicht was standing there, his hawk-like thin face wrinkled in disdain at what he saw within.

---

3. Slang word for contraceptives.

'Enough!' Habicht cried. 'Get rid of the whore. I want to speak to you.'

Schulze shrugged eloquently at Chink. 'You, take the Hungarian lady back where you found her. She'll have to come back later to do my washing and sewing!'

The Hungarian whore looked from him to Schulze, then shook her head as if in complete bewilderment. As she went out, Schulze savoured the wonderful mechanical action of the girl's buttocks, as she wriggled down the little street. Then sadly he began to pull on his 'dice-beakers,' while *Obersturmbannführer* Habicht tapped his pistol holster with his fingers impatiently, as if time were running out very fast.

THREE

Together the Regimental Commander and big Sergeant-Major walked down the lines of the *Europa*, speaking little but noting the busy activity on all sides with professional eyes. The men were mostly in their teens, poorly trained and probably unable speak anything but their native languages.

For a while they paused at the outskirts of the little town and watched a group of smooth-faced, teenaged lieutenants uder the command of an older captain, whose left arm was in a sling, practising an infantry attack. But they obviously did not know the first thing about how to use the cover of the *Royal Tiger* which was leading the feigned attack. Their 'grape'[1] was too far behind the tank – probably they were too scared to get close enough to its roaring tracks.

In the end Habicht barked: 'Captain, punishment drill for your group. They are very idle and slack!'

The captain did not hesitate. '*Hinlegen!*' he bellowed.

As one the young officers flopped face downwards into the thick grey mud churned up by the tank's tracks.

'*Aufstehen!*'

They sprang to their feet again, their uniforms grey and soaked with mud.

---

1. An attack formation used in conjunction with a tank.

'*Hinlegen!*' the captain barked again and they fell to the ground once more like a series of wooden puppets.

'Straight from Bad Tolz cadet school,' Habicht commented. 'Seventeen year olds, the lot of 'em. Four months ago, they were still rubbing the seats of their trousers shiny in high school.'

'Sir.' Schulze said, but nothing more. He was wondering why he had been picked out for this guided tour of *SS Regiment Europa*'s weaknesses and deficiencies.

Habicht seemed to be able to read his mind. He suddenly said, 'Probably you are wondering why I am showing you all this, Schulze?'

'Sir.'

'I shall tell you. The great days are long past when we of the Armed SS got the cream of the Fatherland's new recruits. Not a man under one metre eighty, not even accepted if he had a single filling in his teeth. The barrel is about scraped clean. But there is no purpose in complaining about it. We must do what we have to do with what we have – those raw young officers and my Europeans. What they lack in experience and training, they make up for in fervour and their belief in the Folk, Fatherland, and Führer.'

'But that won't stop the Popovs' bullets, sir,' Schulze said.

The light died in Habicht's eye. 'Agreed,' he said as coldly as before. 'That is why I requested *Reichsführer SS Himmler* personally to let me have a cadre of experienced SS NCOs for my regiment. You and your comrades of the *Wotan* form that cadre.'

In silence the two men walked to the shabby one-time synagogue which now served as the *Europa*'s HQ At the door Habicht crooked his linger at one of the two sentries, armed with machine-pistols, and barked, '*Sturmmann*, to my office, guard the door until I have finished my talk with Sergeant-Major Schulze.'

Carefully Habicht locked the door behind a mystified Schulze and pulled the blackout shutters closed before putting on the light, a single fly-blown electric bulb without a shade.

'Schulze,' Habicht began slowly, 'I'm going to tell you some thing which so far I have only told to my senior officers. I'm going to have to rely heavily on you and your Wotan men in what is to come. You have seen the standard of training of my young officers. I'm going to attach two of your veterans to each one of them. They will give him the experienced support he will need. You must give them the necessary motivation. The situation here in Hungary is very grim. Last November, as soon as the mass of the Hungarian Army began surrendering to the Reds, our whole front was forced back to the Danube and the Fatherland threatened anew. Our war economy depends on the Hungarian bauxite and one third of the crude oil we use in the refining industry to make the *Luftwaffe's* aviation spirit comes from this country. As a result we tried to hold on to Budapest and stop the Reds driving any further into Hungary.

'But while our forces were occupied with the task of keep-ing Malinovsky's Army out of Budapest, that damned cunning Tolbuchin moved up from Belgrade and crossed the Danube near its confluence with the Drava. We had not expected the Reds to cross there but they did and driving rapidly north-west to Lake Balaton, they upset the whole German front in Hungary. By Chrismas Eve, the two Armies completed the encirclement of Budapest, cutting off 150,000 of our troops, including comrades of ours of the 8th and 22nd SS Cavalry Divisions.'

Habicht strode over to the big wall map. 'Remember now, Schulze, what I am telling you now is absolutely secret. It will cost you your head if you breathe a word of it to anyone.' Habicht drew himself up proudly. 'Schulze, the German Army in Hungary is going over to the offensive again. The rot has stopped. There will be no more retreats. Soon we march again!'

'General Balck of the 6th Army has decided that with the support of his infantry divisions, we of the *Viking* and our com-rades of the *SS Death's Head Division* will break out without any preliminary artillery or air support from the north – here.' He tapped the map.

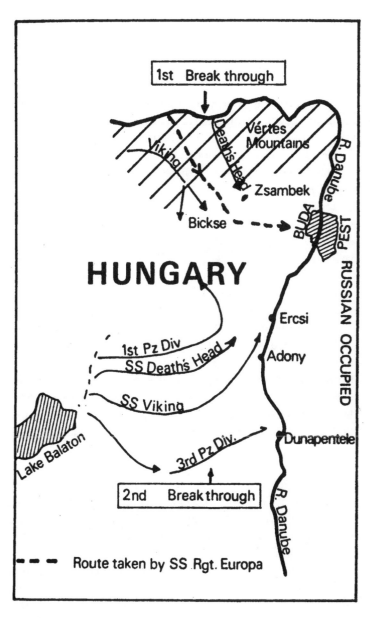

MAP I: The situation in Hungary, 1st January, 1945

'But that's mountain country, sir,' Schulze objected. 'Difficult for tanks and armoured vehicles.'

Habicht beamed at him. 'Exactly! That is why General Balck picked the area for the *4th SS Panzer Corps*. The Reds will never expect us to attack through the mountains, especially in winter. It will be the task of the Viking to roll through the Vértes Mountains and take as its initial objective Bickse, which should place the whole southern Hungarian road network in our hands, a network that is particularly important to German High Command.

'That is where *Europa* comes in. You see General Balck has honoured the Regiment with a special task. *Viking* will have as its initial object Bickse. On our left flank, *Death's Head* will have as its object Zsambek. Both will use the only road network through the mountains to reach those objectives. Accordingly once the Reds tumble to what is going on, they will attempt to block those road networks.

But there is one road through the Vértes Mountains which our Intelligence is sure that they do not know about. And even if they did, they would hardly imagine we would attempt to use it in the depths of winter because it is one thousand metres or more above sea-level, running here,' he tapped the map, 'between the twin objectives. Our object then is to slip in and through the Red lines without their spotting us, until we reach the road network beyond.'

'And then, sir?'

'Then, Schulze, we shall race towards Budapest at the head of the *SS Panzer Corps*.' His hawklike face gleamed with sudden, almost crazy fanaticism. 'Imagine it, Schulze. We will be a symbol of hope and renewed courage for the Fatherland – a symbol for the whole Western World. A regiment of European volunteers sacrificing their blood to save one of Europe's oldest cities from the Bolshevik horde. The Western World will acclaim our success. We start in two days' time. At twenty-two hundred hours on the first of January, 1945.'

'*Happy shitting New Year,*' Schulze thought with a helpless sinking feeling.

FOUR

'*As the New Year begins, my dear Folk Comrades, I should like to thank all of you, men, women and the children of the Hitler Youth for what you have suffered, tolerated, done, achieved. Don't despair! I want you to continue fighting with the utmost fanaticism in this moment of crisis for our nation...*'

Sergeant-Major Schulze let the words of the Führer's New Year message to the nation drone on. 'The Hawk'[1] had insisted that everyone in the Regiment should listen despite the fact that most of the European troops could not understand a word of it.

Moodily Schulze lounged in the lice-infested straw next to Chink and surveyed the young soldiers of his new company, dressed in full battle-kit minus their helmets. The men were pale and tense. They smoked a lot and went often to the evil-smelling thunderboxes at the end of the long barn to urinate. They were scared; after all they were going into action for the first time.

Outside it had been snowing heavily all day long. Schulze could imagine what the roads up in the mountains were going to be like.

---

1. Habicht means 'hawk' in German.

'*I devote every hour to building up the will to resist of my armies, introducing new weapons, forming new divisions. And I assure you, Folk Comrades, our enemies will soon learn that I have not been sleeping...*'

'You shouldn't have bothered to wake up, bastard,' Schulze mumbled under his breath.

'*I cannot close this message without thanking the Lord God on high for the aid he has always given to me and my Folk, which has made us stronger than our enemies...*'

'Bloody hypocrite!' Schulze snorted and pushed aside the black-out curtain.

Half an hour later, *Obersturmbannführer* Habicht stamped through the snow to where Schulze and the Chink were working their way down the long line of waiting vehicles, checking tracks and suspension. In spite of the weather, he was beaming 'You heard the Führer's speech?'

'Sir.'

'Wasn't it magnificent?'

'Sir!' Both of them replied woodenly again.

The Hawk smiled fanatically. 'It would be an honour to die for a man like that.'

Inwardly Schulze groaned, and said: 'We have checked the vehicles' tracks. They're too tight for deep snow. Once we get up there in the mountains –'

The Hawk waved aside his objection. He was in a tremendous mood, almost as if he had been drinking. 'A mere bagatelle, my dear Schulze. We shall get through. Now order of march. I shall give myself the honour of leading in the command halftrack. You will follow in the VW jeep, leading the rest of the halftracks with the grenadiers. Convoy distance between my vehicle and yours will be two hundred metres. Understood?'

Schulze gave a little sigh of relief. At least he was not going to be at point. If the Hawk bought it, he'd be two hundred metres away; that would give him and the Chink a chance of making dust. 'Sir.'

'We'll be in constant radio communication, of course. Therefore if I run into trouble – which I don't anticipate – you will bring up the grenadiers. The Royal Tigers will bring up the rear. I don't want one of those monsters getting into trouble in the snow and blocking the road. When we are through and down on the plain again on the other side, they can then take the lead.'

'If,' Schulz thought grimly.

'All right, Schulze. We have the cover of darkness now almost. It will take us three hours to get to the start line. I suggest you call out the men and mount up.' Suddenly he shot out his one hand and said with surprising formality. '*Hals und Bienbruch, Schulzel.*'[2]

Schulze took it uneasily. The hand was hot with suppressed fervour. '*Hals und Beinbruch, Obersturmbannführer.*'

It was too late now to be afraid. Standing on his command halftrack, head ducked inside his camouflaged hood against the icy wind that blew across the limitless field of snow, Habicht looked at the green glowing dial of his watch. It was almost time to go. The feeling of heady excitement had been replaced by one of controlled happiness, like that of a child who knows he was soon going to receive a present.

Germany was returning to the offensive again. Month after month, the Fatherland had suffered defeat after defeat. Russia, Poland, Rumania, Bulgaria, now Hungary – it seemed that nothing had been able to stop the Red Army. For every battalion the hard-pressed German forces had destroyed, a regiment had appeared; for every tank troop wiped out, a squadron; for every plane, a flight. The Reds seemed to possess an inexhaustible supply of men and material.

Yet Habicht knew they *could* be beaten. Now it was no longer Germany on the march, fighting for some selfish imperialistic gain; it was Europe, striving to stop for good the Red tide which would swamp and drown it, if nothing were done soon.

---

2. Roughly 'happy landings'.

SS Regiment Europa would only be the start. Once Budapest was theirs, their success would bring thousands, hundreds of thousands of eager young men from all over Europe flocking to the silver banner of the SS. By then he might well be dead. But what did his sacrifice matter if the success of his Regiment meant that Young Europe would spring to the Germanic Cause, and put an end to the Reds.

His fingers trembling with excitement, he pulled out his signal pistol. 'One...two...three...' he counted off the seconds in a shaky voice, 'nine...ten.'

His finger crooked round the trigger of the clumsy pistol. A soft plop and then a slight hush. The flare climbed rapidly into the dark night sky and exploded in a burst of bright green.

It was the signal!

All along the long column, the engines of the halftracks, jeeps, tanks burst into noisy, crazy life. Habicht, possessed by an almost uncontrollable excitement, slapped his hand on the driver's shoulder. 'FORWARD! ...WE MARCH!' he cried.

'REGIMENT EUROPA ADVANCE!'

THE MOUNTAIN ROAD

ONE

Dark clouds parted in the moon's path for an instant. Schulze, crouched next to Chink and a couple of Cheeseheads they had brought with them for extra fire-power – in case – caught a quick glimpse of the distant peaks. But it wasn't the scenery that held his attention. It was the little bunker, almost covered by deep snow, to the right of the mountain road, fronted by a very deep drop. Then the moon disappeared beneath the clouds again and an almost total darkness engulfed them.

'What do you think, Chink?' Schulze whispered.

Chink sniffed the air a couple of times like a dog.

'Ivans,' he announced finally. 'Chink can tell. You smell.'

Schulze sniffed. Yes, the little *Hiwi* was right. There were Russians up there in the bunker, as the Hawk had predicted.

Schulze thought for a moment. The Hawk would want to attack – would want a 'sacrifice of blood' – but that was not the way he saw it.

'Listen, we're gonna take out that bunker ourselves. The four of you Cheeseheads will advance to the base of the slope, that's about fifty odd metres from the Popov bunker. Me and Chink here will come in at the same time from the flank. When we're in position, I'll whistle twice. You open up with all you've got. Then –'

Chink beat him to it. His long curved knife gleamed wickedly in the faint light. 'Sergeant-Major and Chink cut throats.' The *Hiwi* giggled.

Next to him the Limburger shuddered.

'All right,' Schulze commanded, 'that's the plan. Let's get on with it. Move yer arses!'

Schulze slid through the snow-heavy bushes, grateful for the mountain wind and flurries of snow muffling their approach. Behind him Chink made no sound whatsoever. Schulze could not even hear him breathing despite the steepness of the ascent to the bunker. He was obviously an expert at this sort of thing. Metre by metre they crawled nearer to the still bunker, silhouetted against the night sky. Had they sentries posted somewhere outside? Schulze asked himself. German sentries would have crawled back into the warmth of the bunker, confident no officer would be around, but the Popovs were different, he knew that. They could endure a tremendous degree of cold, and besides in the Peasants' and Workers' Army it was not unusual for an officer to shoot a common soldier out of hand for the slightest dereliction of duty. Schulze decided there would be Popovs outside somewhere or other.

They were about fifty metres away from the bunker. There was no sound save for the howl of the wind in the firs. Schulze stopped suddenly, as Chink pressed his shoulder firmly. Very deliberately the little *Hiwi* brought his mouth close to Schulze's ear. 'Ivan,' he whispered, 'to right!'

Schulze felt his heart beat more rapidly. Two dark shapes detached themselves from the shadows cast by the trees and plodded across their path in the slow weary manner of infantry men all over the world, carrying out sentry duty in the middle of the night.

'*Shit!*' Schulze cursed to himself. The two sentries were directly to their front. He had to get rid of them before they could tackle the bunker, but the ten or fifteen metres of ground which separated them was devoid of cover. The Popovs would spot them before they managed to cover it. He remembered the Cheeseheads down below. If they opened up, it might well distract the sentries. They might run forward to the edge of the drop to check what was going on. In those few seconds, he and Chink would be on the bunker. A grenade through the door and they would be in. They could worry about the two sentries later.

Schulze straightened himself slowly and whistled shrilly, hoping that the sentries would take the sound for that of some night bird. Nothing happened. Neither the sentries stirred, nor was there any reaction from down below.

Schulze glared at the darkness angrily. Nothing!

He tried again – again nothing.

'They're petrified down there, Chink. They're not gonna move. The Dutch bastards have left us in the lurch!'

Schulze was suddenly seized by an all-consuming rage. He pulled the heavy stick grenade out of his belt, ripped out the china pin and counted *one-two-three*. Then he hurled it over the edge of the drop down to where he imagined his men to be. It was an old trick. But it worked. In the same instant that it exploded in a vicious burst of scarlet just behind the Dutch men's positions, they opened fire in wild, fearsome abandon. The sentries shouted something and ran to the side of the slope. Schulze waited no longer. 'Come on Chink – *at the double!*'

They pelted across the snow and hit the bunker. From inside came the sounds of men stirring in alarm. The door was flung open. Chink moved first. His knife flashed and the Russian gurgled once as it opened his throat from the jugular to the carotid. He went down, drowning in his own blood.

Schulze sprang over his writhing body. A half-naked soldier ran down the narrow corridor screaming. Schulze ripped off a burst with his Schmeisser instinctively. The man jacknifed, a froth of pink foamy blood spraying from his wide-open mouth. Behind him Chink opened the first wooden door to their right, tossed in a grenade and pulled it closed again. The wooden wall seemed to bulge like a live thing. Abruptly the room was full of screams and wild, agonized yells. In a flash, the whole corridor reeked of cordite, blood and death.

The two of them ran on. Another little room to their right, the door wide open. Legs spread wide apart, big body half crouched, Schulze clutched his machine pistol to his right hip and sprayed its occupants as they still lay in their beds, tumbling them out of the crude bunks like beetles from underneath a suddenly upturned stone. It was a massacre.

Chink came running up to him, chest heaving, his knife gleaming scarlet now. 'All gone!' he gasped. 'Chink fix!'

'Good for you, you Siberian shit!' he gasped himself, trying hard to control his harsh breathing. 'Not bad for an honorary Aryan —' Suddenly he remembered the sentries. 'Chink, the other two. Come on!'

Frantically they pelted down the body-littered corridor, out into the open again.

'Over there!' Chink gasped.

The two sentries saw them at the same moment. They fired. Their bullets gouged out spouts of snow just in front of Chink. He fired back. Missed! Schulze tried to stop the frantic pumping of his heart so that he could aim correctly. The snarling hiss of his Schmeisser — a full half-second burst — almost ripped the sentry in two.

It was too much for the other man. With a scream of fear, he flung away his rifle and started to run wildly, floundering through the deep snow towards the safety of the trees. Schulze knew he could not let him get away. He pressed the Schmeisser's trigger. Nothing happened. 'Shit!' he cursed bitterly. The magazine was empty.

The Chink raised his machine pistol and tracer-stitched the darkness. Schulze could see the slugs cutting a crazy pattern around the man's running feet. But they were missing him by a metre or more.

'Lift your muzzle, Chink, for Chrissake!' he urged frantically.

But already it was too late The lone Russian was blundering into the firs, crashing into their green gloom and disappearing from sight.

Slowly, very slowly, Chink lowered his machine pistol and looked at Schulze standing there like some ancient Nordic god, turned to stone, oblivious of the wild fire still coming from the Cheeseheads below. 'You think same me, Sarnt-Major?' he asked reluctantly.

'I think the same, Chink,' Schulze answered equally slowly. 'That Popov bastard will tell them we're coming.'

TWO

Dawn. *SS Regiment Europa* was drawn up on the crest of a ridge, the young troopers drinking steaming hot canteens of Muckefuck[1] and washing down the hard Army bread, stamping their feet continually on the packed snow of the road trying to drive out the cold.

Chink filled Schulze's canteen once more with the boiling hot, black brew, and taking the little bottle out of his pocket, poured a quick and generous slug of the fiery Hungarian plum schnaps into the coffee.

'That's the stuff to give the troops, Chink,' Schulze said happily. 'You're not a bad sort – for a foreigner.'

The little man beamed. 'Chink your friend,' he said.

Schulze moved across the snow to where the Hawk was standing, smoking a cigarette and chatting to Major Kreuz, his second-in-command, a tall, rather cynical veteran with an intelligent face adorned by a monocle.

Once Schulze had joined them the Hawk got to the point at once. 'Now I know you are worried, Schulze, that the Red who escaped last night might nave alerted his masters that we are on this road.'

'Sir.'

---

1. Ersatz coffee.

'I appreciate your concern for the safety of our mission, but really where could the man have gone to? I mean we are at least twenty kilometres behind their lines by now and there is still no sign of the man who got away or any other Red unit for that matter.'

'I don't know about that, sir,' Schulze answered doggedly.

'But those fellows in the bunker back there must have had some means of communicating with their HQ.'

'Agreed, Sergeant-Major.' Kreuz spoke for the first time. 'But even if he did somehow manage to get in touch with his people, do you really think that they could do anything to stop us now?' He pointed an elegantly gloved hand to his right. 'Look down there.'

Thin, dark, graceful plumes of smoke were ascending slowly to the sky on the far horizon. Occasionally there was a silent pink ripple, which Schulze knew of old was the explosion of a heavy gun.

'The Viking,' Kreuz said casually, 'giving the Reds a taste of their own medicine for a change.'

'Yes,' the Hawk said. 'The lower road is surely in our hands by now and the Reds will have enough to do without worrying about us up here.'

The Hawk seemed blind to the disaster that could overtake them; packed on one tight winding road like this, they were easy meat for a Russian flank attack. The armoured vehicles would have no room at all to manoeuvre.

'We present more of a threat to them once we're out of these mountains than does the rest of the Division down there,' Schulze persisted. 'Once they find out we're up here, surely they'll do their damn best to stop us.'

Kreuz nodded his approval slowly. 'You are right there, Schulze. There's obviously a brain working somewhere up there in your big turnip.' He smiled cynically at Schulze through his gold-rimmed monocle.

Schulze bristled. 'Some of us sub-human other-rankers have been known to have an idea now and again,' he retorted acidly.

Habicht intervened: 'Kreuz, you seriously think, as obviously Schulze here does, that we might be in trouble?'

'Colonels think, majors carry out orders,' Kreuz answered and then added hastily, 'Yessir. It is possible.'

The Hawk breathed out hard and made a decision. 'All right, you are our explosives expert. Where could you block this road behind us and how long would it take?'

Kreuz ran an expert eye down the length of road that lay behind them, checking the steep slope to the near side for the overhang he would need. Then he spotted it. About three hundred metres back. To the right, the mountainside went down almost sheer. To the left, there was an overhang obviously the work of unskilled engineers – some three metres above the road and jutting out a good two metres. The overhang was obviously unstable – a standing invitation for a landslide.

'There, sir,' Kreuz said. 'With a bit of luck, we could sheer off ten metres of that overhang and block the whole damn road.'

'How long would it take?' Habicht rapped.

'We have no power tools. But if I had enough men working in shifts of ten minutes, boring into the rock flat out, probably about three hours.'

The Hawk glanced at his watch. 'I'll give you exactly ninety minutes – and you've got the whole Regiment at your disposal, save the lookouts. All right, Kreuz, what the hell are you waiting for!'

Schulze almost liked the Hawk at that moment.

In spite of the biting cold on the mountainside, the young men sweated as they slammed the heavy sledge-hammers against the chisels held against the rockface. Time and time again, feet braced against the rock, leg muscles screaming out with the strain, of standing at the forty-five degree angle.

But Schulze did not give them an opportunity to slacken off. He was here, there and everywhere, cursing, cajoling, threatening the gasping young men with cries that most of them did not understand. But if they did not understand the words; Schulze's gestures and grimaces were unmistakable. They toiled on.

Now some of Schulze's own concern had infected Kreuz. Already he had a group of troopers stacking the TNT and nitro-starch blocks under his direction, while the wire, its leads checked for cleanliness, was unreeled along the side of the road, ready for attaching.

An hour passed. Now the holes were about finished. Kreuz began to pass out the charges. The young troopers cradled them carefully to their chests and inserted them delicately into the apertures. Kreuz attached the detonating wire and swiftly checked the leads of the wire with the galvanometer. The little green needle flicked across the dial, swung back and flicked up again.

'The splices are all right. The whole circuit is functioning.' Hurriedly he clamped the wires into the detonating apparatus, while the Hawk glanced impatiently at his watch. He screwed the clamps tight, and straightened up. 'We're all ready, *Obersturm!*' he cried.

The Hawk wasted no time. He clasped his one hand to his mouth and bellowed: 'All right, all you men back round the curve to the vehicles!'

Kreuz kneeling at the little machine next to Schulze glanced back at them and was satisfied everyone was under sufficient cover. He took a deep breath and seizing the wooden-handled plunger pressed it down with one smooth thrust. For a moment nothing seemed to happen. Then there was a series of sharp cracklings like fireworks exploding. The earth beneath their feet began to tremble and suddenly the whole side of the mountain erupted in volcanic fury, scarlet flame, interspersed by brilliant white flashes shot into the sky, followed a moment later by a great spout of earth and rock.

Schulze opened his mouth to prevent his eardrums bursting and felt the hot wave of blast strike him like a flabby fist across the face. For a fleeting second he closed his eyes. When he opened them again, the explosion was over and its roar, diminishing by the instant, was disappearing down the valley, its echo growing fainter and fainter.

The explosives had clawed the whole length of the overhang down. Now the rocks and boulders ripped from the raw new face of the mountain blocked some thirty metres or more of the road in a huge heap, which would take days to clear.

Kreuz broke the heavy silence. 'Well, my friend, there is no way up for the Russians now, that is for sure.'

'Yes, Major,' Schulze answered slowly, 'and no way back for us either.'

THREE

Colonel-General Zacharov, Commander of the Fourth Guards Army, was sweating heavily. Every time he attempted to dry himself with his handkerchief, soaked in cheap *eau-de-cologne*, the field telephone rang and one of the anxious staff officers would pass on the news of the latest disaster. Then the Guards General would break out sweating once more.

Marshal Tolbuchin, Commander of the Second Ukrainian Front, sitting in the corner of the one-time Hungarian villa, which now served as Zacharov's headquarters in the Battle for Budapest, smoked steadily, his broad peasant face expressionless. But he was thinking hard, undisturbed by the regular thump-thump of a gun less than two hundred metres away.

He knew that the Fritz defenders of the Hungarian capital would never be able to break out now. His concern was the new situation to the west. Where in the Holy Virgin's name had the Germans found the strength to launch this morning's surprise attack? What was their objective? Budapest? Or to drive through his axis with the Third Ukrainian Army south of Budapest? Or was it just a spoiling attack – a last desperate attempt by the Fritzes to forestall the Soviet capture of Budapest and the drive into Western Hungary? So many questions, Tolbuchin told himself, and so few answers.

With a heavy groan, he rose to his feet and strolled with deliberate slowness to the centre of the room. The staff officers made way for him like shoals of little fish parting to let some great predatory shark through. Zacharov looked at his superior uneasily, his face ugly and damp with sweat.

Tolbuchin let him wait. The Colonel-General was losing his nerve, he told himself. If he didn't master this day's crisis he would sack him...or worse. Marshal Stalin did not take too kindly to Army Commanders who allowed themselves to be defeated. Finally he breathed out a slow ring of blue smoke and said: 'Well, Comrade General?'

Zacharov jabbed a finger at the big map spread out on the table in front of him. 'The whole line of my Thirty-First Guards Rifle Corps between Naszaly-Tata and Felsogalla has been broken into, Comrade Marshal. Their objectives seem to be – from north to south – Gran, Zsambek and Bickse.'

'Bickse?' Tolbuchin spoke for the first time.

'Yes, Comrade Marshal. Felsogalla has already been taken by the Fritzes on the road to Bickse. It is obvious that it is one of their main objectives.'

Unceremoniously the burly Marshal pushed the sweating Army Commander out of the way and bending over the map, scrutinized it keenly for a moment. He rose and announced quite simply, 'Budapest.'

The door at the far end of the big echoing room was suddenly flung open and Colonel Zis, Zacharov's Intelligence Officer, entered, escorting a private soldier. The man was in a terrible state, his earth-brown tunic was ripped and torn, while there was a dull stain on the right side of his baggy breeches and a ragged hole which indicated that a bullet had entered his leg.

'What is this?' Zacharov demanded angrily.

'Comrade General, one of the retreating units of the Fifth Guards Cavalry picked him two hours ago not far from Zsambek.'

'And?'

'Well, Comrade General, he belonged to a small guard unit, whose task it was to cover the mountain road through the Vértes

Range. Last night, the outpost was overrun by the Fritzes – SS armour, he thinks.

'What?' Zacharov exploded. 'Not that too!'

'Vodka,' Marshal Tolbuchin snapped, clicking his fingers. The ever-present aide produced a silver flask of the fiery spirit and placed it into the Marshal's waiting hand.

'Drink a drop, little brother. It will warm you up.'

The soldier blinked his eyes rapidly – a Marshal of the Soviet Union offering him a drink from his own flask and calling him 'little brother!' He seized the flask and took a swift, deep slug

Tolbuchin inwardly told himself he must have the flask sterilized. 'All right, comrade, now tell me what happened on the mountain road last night?'

The sole survivor of Schulze's raid on the bunker told his story in a hurried, nervous manner.

'So comrades,' Tolbuchin said when the man had been dismissed, 'that confirms it. The Fritzes want Bickse because it is the centre of the road network which they will use to drive on Budapest.'

Zacharov looked at him aghast.

Tolbuchin ignored the look. 'Now, it is clear that the first threat is this Fritz unit which will spearhead the attack on Budapest across the mountain range.'

'But we have nothing to stop them, Comrade Marshal,' Zacharov objected hastily, already visualizing 'Old Leather Face' (as the Army called Stalin behind his back) ordering him to one of his Siberian concentration camps for 'lack of Soviet zeal'. 'How can one get armour up into those mountains in this kind of weather?'

'The Fritzes obviously managed to get armour through, Comrade General,' Tolbuchin said mildly enough. 'So you've got no reserves, eh?' He considered for a moment and then demanded to be connected with Headquarters, Second Ukrainian Front.

'Comrade Major Suslov to the phone – at once,' he commanded.

'*The Grey Eagle!*' Zacharov breathed.

Tolbuchin looked at the heavy-set, sweating Guards Army Commander with undisguised contempt, then Suslov's cheerful, confident voice was at the other end and he was rapping out his instructions in sharp little staccato phrases.

The Grey Eagle listened in silence, before saying, 'You realize Comrade Marshal that you are probably condemning about half my Eagles to death with an operation like this in that terrain and in this weather?'

There was no change in the cheerful, confident note in Suslov's voice. 'Probably,' the Marshal answered. 'But they will die for the glory of the Red Army and the Soviet Union.'

The Grey Eagle made an obscene suggestion about what he could do with such glory, and hung up without another word.

For the first time that long grim January day, Marshal of the Soviet Union Tolbuchin smiled.

FOUR

It had been a back-breaking day for the young men of *SS Regiment Europa*, as they had fought their way through the blinding snowstorms higher and higher into the mountains. Each new curve in the winding road had been a minor engineering feat, as the vehicles, sliding and skidding on the slick new snow, had been dragged round by sheer muscle-power, with hundreds of freezing, cursing, yelling SS men digging a new path for them in the rock and snow.

Now the Regiment was stuck again. At the head of the column, just behind Habicht's command vehicle which had cleared the corner safely, a halftrack full of grenadiers had begun to slip towards the sheer drop on the far side of the road and the ashen-faced driver had only managed to bring the ten ton vehicle to stop at the very edge of the drop. Behind it the whole Regiment was stalled again, the drivers gunning their engines nervously, while they waited for the obstruction to be cleared away.

Angrily Habicht pushed by the young driver and strode to the side of the road to gaze down at the drop. With his good foot, he stamped on snow-covered ground there, obviously to test the strength of the rock below the snow.

'Schulze, get a dozen men at each side of the vehicle ready to push when I give the word.'

'Over the side?' Schulze asked.

'No. Back on to the road,' the Hawk said. He swung himself up into the cab just vacated by the shaken driver. 'I'll get the bitch out myself.'

Hurriedly Schulze ordered the men to their positions on both sides of the halftrack, while the Hawk gunned the motor and then gently let out the clutch. The wheel trembled violently in his single hand. With a lurch the halftrack moved forward a little as he put his foot on the accelerator.

'Put yer backs into it!' Schulze yelled, as the troopers took the strain. They heaved. The halftrack moved forward a little more, its rear tracks throwing up a shower of stone and snow. Another lurch. Abruptly the track hit ice or hard-packed snow. The vehicle lost traction. The tracks whirled furiously, the Hawk gunning the engine all out.

'*Pass op!*' one of the men on the sides yelled in panic.

The Dutchmen jumped clear as the halftrack began to swing to one side,

'Get back there, you Cheeseheads!' Schulze cried in dismay, as the men scattered out of the path of the vehicle which was sliding sideways towards the edge of the road, the Hawk fighting the wheel crazily.

Schulze jumped out of its path just as Habicht regained control of the halftrack, preventing it from sliding that last couple of paces on the treacherous granulated snow.

'Get out, sir!' Schulze yelled from where he lay sprawled in the snow. 'Let it go over the side. The bastard's not worth −'

The words died on his lips. Quite deliberately the Hawk rammed home first gear again. Gently, very gently, he let out the clutch, the engine whining in protest as he did so. The halftrack lurched forward again. Schulze held his breath. If it slipped now, the Hawk would not have a chance. His face showed no fear, just anger that this piece of metal would not obey his commands. He increased his pressure on the accelerator, thick clouds of blue smoke pouring from the halftrack's exhaust. Still the vehicle did not respond. Schulze watched, his mouth wide open, his heart beating frantically in an onslaught of panic. *Would he do it?*

Suddenly the track caught. Habicht did not hesitate. He swung the wheel a half turn to the left. For a moment he thought he had done the wrong thing. Desperately he gave the vehicle more power. The halftrack jolted forward. He swung the wheel round. The tracks answered readily. A moment later he was away from the danger of the mountainside, the vehicle righted and pointing up the slope once again.

On the ground, Schulze breathed out hard. The Hawk might be out to kill them, with his blind belief in Germany's cause, but he was a damned brave man all the same.

But there was no time for congratulations. For in that same instant that Habicht sprang lightly from the halftrack's cab as if nothing special had occurred, there was the faint throb of a light aeroplane's motor, increasing by the second, coming towards them from the east.

'It's a sewing machine all right,'[1] Kreuz said, shading his eyes against the angled yellow glare of the dying sun.

Crouched behind the cover of the leading halftrack, the Hawk and Schulze watched the little biplane coming ever closer to their positions. 'With a bit of luck, Schulze,' Habicht said, 'he might not spot us. It's already getting dark and those firs up there cast quite a bit of shadow over the road.'

A moment later the Rata was over them, trailing a gigantic black shadow behind it over the snow. Swiftly the two men rolled over and saw it disappear over the nearest peak. Habicht breathed out a sigh of relief. 'The Red didn't –' He stopped short. Behind the peak there was the sound of the little reconnaissance plane turning. 'It's coming back!'

---

1. German soldier's name for the Rata reconnaissance plane, given to it because of the noise its engine made.

'He's spotted us!' Schulze cried in alarm. 'You flak gunners get on to him!'

Desperately the crew of the quadruple flak, mounted on one of the halftracks, scrambled for their gun, just as the Rata appeared from behind the mountain, coming in very low. At a hundred metres, it began to fly the length of the column, while the frantic-fingered gunners fumbled with their gun. Angrily, Schulze let fly with a futile burst from his Schmeisser. Suddenly the four slim barrels of the 20mm flak opened up with a tremendous burst. White tracer slit the blue sky furiously. The Russian pilot reacted at once. His speed rose as he opened up the throttle. Suddenly he banked to the left, leaving the angry stream of shells to hiss by him harmlessly, some twenty metres away and a moment later he was gone, leaving the furious sweating gunners firing purposely at the empty sky.

The firing died away and there was no sound save the soft throb of the plane's engine to the east, getting fainter by the second.

Schulze broke the silence: 'Looks to me like trouble, sir. If they can't come on up after us because of the road block, they can plant a nasty surprise for us at the other end now they definitely know we're here.

'Yes, I suppose you're right, Schulze,' the Hawk said a little wearily. 'But we'll face up to that particular problem when we come to it. Tell the men to mount up again, would you please?'

But before long Sergeant Major Schulze was going to be proved wrong, very seriously wrong indeed.

FIVE

'*Helmets on!*' Major Suslov barked above the roar of the towing plane.

Suslov, a tall dark officer in his late twenties, looked along the dim, green-lit length of the big glider and nodded his approval. His Grey Eagles, not one of them over twenty-five and virtually every one of them decorated in combat, looked fit and confident in spite of the terrible danger of their bold mission.

'Check equipment!' he snapped.

With the precision of machines, each man turned to his neighbour and checked his equipment – Machine pistol, ammunition, grenades, smoke and high explosive, pistol, emergency rations – before reporting 'All correct'.

'Comrade Major.' Suslov turned. It was the young glider pilot, who like all the pilots in the Grey Eagle Battalion had been a pre-war Soviet champion in the *Komosol* Youth Movement.

'Yes?'

'The tugs are preparing to drop the tow now.'

Suslov swung round and faced his men. 'Prepare for landing!' he ordered.

Veterans that they were, the young men adopted the landing posture – hands clasping the metal spars behind their heads, feet raised slightly from the floor – immediately. There was a light tug. The glider shuddered slightly as the pilot brought up the nose in order to brake. Suddenly there was silence as the towing plane broke off in a great curve and began heading back east. All noise died away. The January dawn seemed suddenly unbelievably calm and peaceful. Now the Grey Eagles could do nothing but wait and rely on the pilot to put them down safely on the difficult terrain.

Major Suslov had been instrumental in setting up the first experimental glider company of paratroop volunteers, from which the Grey Eagles had sprung. From the war against Finland right through the terrible battles against the Germans in '41 and '42 on to the great victories of the last two years, the Grey Eagles had always been in the forefront of the action. Time and time again the Battalion had been decimated in some desperate action behind enemy lines, but always there had been more than enough volunteers to fill its empty ranks again. Suslov and his Grey Eagles were, after all, the idols of Soviet youth. Had not Stalin publicly embraced Suslov at a Kremlin reception in front of the newsreel cameras and called him 'the boldest of the bold?'

Suslov, however, was not a reckless commander. It was only because of the desperate situation of Zacharov's Guards Army that he had allowed himself to be talked into landing his Eagles on the most difficult type of terrain possible – the mountains.

Anxiously he pushed his way down the littered gangway to where Boris, a flaxen-haired Ukrainian crouched over the controls, swinging the glider round in a huge circle to lower its speed, prior to landing.

On the western horizon the darkness was breaking up, turning to the threatening opaque grey, which he knew was snow falling far away. But Suslov had not eyes for the horizon. His gaze was fixed on the ground below, it looked far from promising. Long stretches of dark green, which were firs, broken at regular intervals by sharp, naked peaks. 'What do you think Boris?' he asked, after glancing upwards to check that the rest of the Battalion's gliders were there.

'It's not good,' the pilot answered, not taking his eyes from his controls.

Suslov could see the faint line of sweat fringing the pilot's hairline and knew that if one of the Soviet Union's most experienced pilots was beginning to sweat, they were in for trouble.

Boris straightened the big glider. There was no sound now save the hiss of the wind, as the glider came down at speed. The nose-dive brakes were applied and the fuselage trembled violently. The ground loomed up ever larger, steep and littered with what seemed gigantic snowballs. 'Boulders!' Boris cried in alarm.

'*Crash landing!*' Suslov yelled back into the plane. The Grey Eagles tensed their bodies, but their young faces showed no fear.

The ground was racing by them now at a tremendous speed. Boris flung up the nose and the next instant, two thousand pounds of glider and men hit the snowy slope. Snow sprayed up on both sides of them higher than the cockpit, in a blinding white stream. Wood and canvas splintered and tore. The barbed wire they had wrapped around the skids to shorten the breaking distance snapped like bits of wet string as it hit the boulders concealed beneath the snow. The skids squeaked shrilly, as the glider slewed towards the edge of a precipice. Boris, fighting the controls frantically, brought the glider round just in time. The glider slithered away, lurched against a huge boulder and came to an abrupt stop.

'Good man, Boris,' Suslov cried and slapped him on the back. 'All right, my Eagles – *out,*' he yelled.

At once the glider's interior was transformed into a frenzy of movement. The Eagles sprang to their feet. With their heavy boots, those who were too far from the open door smashed through the canvas, as they had been trained to do, and stumbled out into the cold dawn air, to form a defensive perimeter.

Suslov checked his positions and stared up at the sky. The others were coming in now, ten gliders bearing the rest of the Battalion. The first one hissed over his head. It came into a perfect landing, nose held high, brakes screaming in shrill protest as it shrieked to a stop in a gleaming white flurry of snow. An instant later his

Eagles came tumbling out. The second one followed closely but number three hit the ground hard and began to slide across the hard-packed snow. Brakes screaming all out, trailing a great wake of snow behind it, the glider shot helplessly over the edge of the precipice and fell over one thousand metres, a broken-off wing falling behind it to its death like a lone leaf.

All the others landed safely after this disaster. The Grey Eagles had pulled off the most difficult landing in the history of glider-borne operations. They had landed on a snow-covered mountain range, some five thousand metres above sea level!

'It looks as if we'll go down in the history books after the war, Comrade Major,' Boris commented as the Grey Eagles began to form up.

Major Suslov looked up from his map for a moment, and grinned. 'We've got to survive it first, Boris.'

Thirty minutes later, the men of the Soviet Union's élite unit had disappeared into the firs on their way to their confrontation with *SS Regiment Europa*. Soon the battle of the giants would begin.

SIX

As the morning of the second day in the mountains progressed, the snow steadily began to fall more thickly. The wind increased too. Now the long line of vehicles, crawling through the Vértes Mountains, battled against a veritable blizzard, the lookouts' faces stung by the flying snow, their eyebrows white with the bitter crystals. The road ran through steep-sided gorges, its edge hanging vertiginously over the valley below.

Despite the treacherous conditions *Obersturmbannführer* Habicht was exceedingly pleased. It was over fifteen hours since the little Russian reconnaissance plane had spotted them. By now he could have expected the first Red attack from the air. But in this weather the Reds would not be able to fly. And even if they could, their pilots would have a devil of a job spotting the convoy on this particular stretch of the road, with the great sheer mountain side giving them the cover they need.

'You look very pleased with yourself, *Obersturmbannführer*,' Kreuz remarked, cleaning the snow off his monocle, and wishing himself in Berlin with a glass of steaming hot grog.

'I am,' Habicht replied 'In spite of the weather we are making excellent time. Another day, in my estimation, and we should be through the mountains. Then the road to Budapest should be wide open for us.'

'Providing that the *Viking* and *Death's Head* keep up their attack-schedule,' Kreuz objected mildly.

'But they are, my dear Kreuz,' Habicht answered. He indicated the chattering command radio at the back of the halftrack, with its freezing operator crouched over it. 'Division signalled an hour ago that the *Viking* is making progress all along the front. The first day went splendidly and we're doing just as well today. We caught the Reds with their pants well and truly down yesterday.'

'Excellent!' Kreuz said with hollow enthusiasm.

'Besides,' Habicht continued, 'even if the Division weren't making such splendid progress, I would go on.'

Kreuz looked at him aghast. '*Alone?*'

'Alone,' Habicht echoed, a faint smile on his thin lips. 'You see we are a symbol, we of the *Europa*.' He paused moment airily, as if he were first having to convince himself of the truth of what he was about to say. 'And sometimes symbols are more effective when those who create them are...are dead, don't you think?'

Kreuz shivered. Now he knew the Hawk was insane.

Otto Habicht had decided on that day in the peaceful little SS Cavalry Hospital in Heidelberg that he was not going to survive the war. He had done so quietly and completely undramatically in the stillness of the big summer-white room, with the only sound of the barges on the Neckar outside to disturb the sterile hospital calm. It had not been the loss of his lower leg which had caused him to come to his overwhelming decision. It had been the other thing.

SS Oberstabsarzt Phelps had broken it gently to him when he felt the sudden strangeness between his legs after the three day series of operations on his lower body. At first, he had hidden his terrible revelation behind medical terminology:

'Wounds in the scrotal sack...inguinal canal...removal of sin and dex...' Habicht had interrupted him coldly: 'Have you taken my balls off, doctor?'

Numbly Phelps had nodded.

'Am I a eunuch now?'

'Yes, both dex and sin – I mean right and left testicles were irreparably injured by the mortar burst which took off your lower leg. I'm afraid there was nothing else I could do…' his voice had tailed away. There was nothing more he could say to the man lying on the simple white bed in front of him.

Habicht had thanked him gravely for saving his life, asked him to leave and considered the situation as any other military problem, weighing the pros and cons, considering the possibilities – the inability to marry, the inevitable accumulation of more and more fat, the increasingly high-pitched voice, the female instability of the eunuch. He had come to his decision. Before the war ended, he would die – grandly – in some desperate bold venture at the head of his men as befitted a Habicht, whose family had served Prussia since the days of the Great Frederick himself. Now as his regiment ground its way ever higher into the Vértes Mountains, Colonel Habicht knew this was that desperate, bold venture he had promised himself.

The Grey Eagles had been climbing steadily for over three hours, plodding upwards in strained silence, weighed down with thirty kilos of equipment per man. There was no sound, save the squeak of their frozen boots on the packed snow and sharp exhalations of breath.

But ahead of them Suslov knew they were coming to the end of their march. Before them the key height, which dominated the mountain road, loomed ever larger. He had chosen it because of its excellent strategic position. Behind it to the north, there was a sheer rockwall. To the east and south it was bounded by a ravine, narrow but very deep. In both directions there was an excellent field of fire. To the west, it overlooked the road the Fritzes must take if they were to break out of the mountains. From the point of view of defence, the height could not have been better situated. Once established on top of it, a handful of men, well dug-in and determined, could hold off an army.

Suslov knew his men needed a rest badly – they had been going with only one ten minute stop since the drop – but he knew too he could not let them halt. They had to be in position on the height before the Fritzes arrived. 'Grey Eagles,' he cried, feeling the icy mountain air stab at his lungs like a sharp knife, 'at the double!' He pumped his clenched fist up and down twice swiftly: the infantry signal for 'at the double'.

Eyes glazed, yet determined, the paras stumbled after him.

Obersturmbannführer Habicht also looked eagerly towards the gleaming white peak, knowing that it was the highest point in the Vértes. Once it was passed, the going would be downhill, a straight run to the floor of the valley and the vital road network beyond.

He urged on his column, taking risks on the surface of the mountain road, which he would not have dared to that morning. '*Tempo…tempo*,' he barked over and over again into the radio which linked him with Schulze's VW jeep. 'Get those men moving, Sarnt-Major!'

Schulze hurried the rest of the convoy along like an angry sheepdog, switching in and out of the ponderous halftracks with the little jeep, taking appalling risks as he wheeled back and forth. At his side, a fearful Chink, his face now a sickly green, could do nothing but close his slant eyes and groan, 'Sarnt-Major, you think Hamburg, eh, and fucki-fucki shop after big war!'

Habicht's tactics paid off. Even the hard-pressed young drivers, virtually exhausted by the terrible conditions through which they had been forced to drive these last thirty-six hours, seemed to be infected by the Commander's enthusiasm. They, too, started handling the clumsy dangerous half tracks, as if they were light racing cars, accelerating just before they came to a bend, changing down with a crash – right across the gated gear box – and swinging round it with only the merest tap on the brake pedal, ignoring the frightening swing of the vehicle's rump towards the off-side edge of the mountain road and the awesome drop.

The height to their right loomed ever larger in their worn, red-rimmed eyes. Soon they would reach it.

Suslov plodded determinedly through the deep snow at the top of the height. Everywhere his Eagles were digging in, forming large walls of snow, broken by firing slits, opening their flies to urinate with a hot hiss onto the walls so that when the surface of the suddenly melting snow refroze, it would form a solid sheet of ice to ward off any stray slug.

The skilled airborne men had formed a three-sided perimeter of some 200 metres in length, with its open, undefended end towards the sheer, naked rockwall – so sheer, indeed that even the blizzard which was abating had not lodged any snow on its surface. It was an excellent position, easily defensible even if the weather improved sufficiently for the Fritzes to call up an air strike. He was confident that he could withstand anything the Germans threw at him.

He paused at the twin mortars set up in the centre of the perimeter, next to the big snow-covered boulder which he had chosen as his own command post. The mortarmen were busy rubbing more winterized grease on the sights of the weapons and the levels they used to judge their firing angles. '*Horoscho*, my Eagles,' he complimented them on their foresight. 'You are thinking well.'

Sergei Kolchak looked up at his commander: 'And what are we going to call this mountain, Comrade Commander?' he demanded.

Suslov's gaze fell on the Grey Eagles' battalion flag, thrust into the snow by the boulder command post: a grey eagle against a bright red background, its claws extended, its cruel beak ready to tear its prey.

'There you are, Kolchak, there's your name for you.'

'What, Comrade Commander?'

'Why, Grey Eagle Mountain!'

Kolchak beamed, 'Of course,' he breathed.

'Comrade Commander.'

Suslov swung round. It was Oleg, the battalion runner. 'What is it?' he snapped, the flag forgotten now, at the sight of the urgent look on Oleg's face.

'The Fritzes, Comrade Commander – they're coming up the road!' He doubled to the edge of the perimeter with Oleg. Together they flopped into the snow.

Down below the first evil snout of a halftrack had begun to nose its way round the bend in the road on the last stretch before it surmounted the pass. Suslov focused his binoculars hastily, taking care to shade the lenses with one hand to avoid giving away his position.

The men, crowded in what was obviously the command vehicle, sprang into his vision. He knew immediately from the camouflaged overalls they were the SS, the hated Fritz killers. His attention was captured by the man with the eye patch, hood flung back to reveal the cap with its death's head badge. Suslov allowed his glasses to rest for a moment on the man's haughty, emaciated face and knew instinctively that this was the commander. He would be the man they would kill first.

Swiftly he squirmed back through the deep snow and doubled back to the waiting mortarmen. 'All right,' he barked, 'we've got Fritzes to kill at last!'

Habicht leaned forward over the top of the driving cab, urging the halftrack up those last hundred metres to the top of the pass, his mind racing with plans. Once he had the Regiment over the pass he would race through the night down the mountain, taking whatever roadblock the Reds might have set up for him on the exit to the valley by surprise. After that, it would be only a mere twenty kilometres to the Hungarian capital. He swallowed hard, hardly daring to believe it was possible that by this time on the following day he might be in Budapest.

'More speed, driver!' he commanded harshly.

'I'm doing my best, sir,' the driver answered, 'but it's –'

His words were silenced by a soft plop up ahead. Then another and another. An instant later the plops became an obscene, stomach-churning howl.

'*What the hell...!*' Habicht cried in alarm and stared upwards at the little puffs of white smoke on the high peak to their right and the small black objects hurtling towards them. Then he realized what they were. 'MORTARS!' he yelled.

Frantically the driver attempted to stop; but to no avail – the halftrack would not respond in the icy surface. The next instant, the first salvo of mortar bombs from the peak straddled them. One exploded directly in front of the halftrack, sending up a huge spurt of snow, coloured a brilliant scarlet. A second sailed harmlessly over the edge of the precipice, but the third bomb struck the road just under the skidding halftrack's front axle. The ten-ton vehicle reared into the air like a bucking horse put to the saddle for the first time. Glass splintered. Metal shrieked. Habicht, the veteran, turned his head away from the hot blast, laden with gleaming razor-sharp fragments of steel just in time. His driver was not so quick.

The fist-sized piece of red-hot steel hissed through the cab window and took the top of his head off as neatly as any surgeon performing a trepan. The boy screamed just once. Then with his brains tumbling out of his head, his lifeless body lurched limp against the wheel. The command halftrack smashed into the mountainside and came to an abrupt stop, fifty metres from the top of the pass.

The Battle of Grey Eagle Mountain had begun.

THE BATTLE OF GREY EAGLE MOUNTAIN

ONE

On Friday morning, 4 January, 1945, Marshal Tolbuchin sacked Zacharov and took over the defence of the River Danube line himself.

Under the present circumstances his demoralized Guards could not conceivably stop the *Royal Tigers* of the two élite SS Panzer divisions which were leading the German thrust through the mountains. But the further the Fritzes penetrated into the Vértes Range, the longer and more exposed their flanks became. His first order to his Guards Cavalry, the most mobile and most flexible of his units in mountainous terrain, read simply: 'Tickle the German's ribs for him so he loses control of his head!'

Thus his cavalry regiments began a day-long series of bloody little hit-and-run raids along the Germans' long, exposed flanks, forcing the *4th SS Panzer Corps* to detach more and more emergency units to protect the flanks, and by doing so weakening the point.

Tolbuchin's next order went to the commander of the troops attacking Budapest itself. If the city fell, he reasoned that the steam might go out of the German attack. A sizeable number of German troops within the capital would be Soviet prisoners, and the relief forces would realize that they were shedding their blood for an objective already in Russian hands.

The second order was as simple as the first, but far more brutal. It read: 'Take Budapest soon or face the consequences.' Every regular Soviet officer had long known what the 'consequences' were, ever since the Great Army Purge of 1938: the camps or the firing squad. The General would understand.

His third order took more time to carry out. It went to every artillery commander on the long Second Ukrainian Front Command. It read: 'I want every spare artillery piece, mortar, anti-tank gun rushed to the Budapest front *immediately*.'

During that grey morning, Tolbuchin's staff built up a great barrier of artillery in front of the advancing SS, ranging from the smallest mortar to the fearsome 'Katuschka' rocket batteries. By midday the artillery was ready to go into action, albeit without a co-ordinated fire plan. But a fire plan was not needed in the rugged mountain territory. All the local artillery commander needed was to wait for the first SS tank to appear around the bend to his front and then call down the whole weight of fire at his disposal upon it.

Slowly but surely, the burly Marshal's measures began to pay off. *SS Panzer Division Viking* managed to capture Vétes-Tolna that morning, but found it difficult to get out of the village and push on eastwards. *SS Panzer Division Death's Head* captured one of its key objectives that same morning – Tarjan, but when it tried to link up with Balck's infantry, which had made a successful assault crossing of the Danube to its right, the Division found its advance barred by massed Soviet artillery. Now the SS was measuring its progress eastwards in metres, instead of the kilometres of the day before.

There was only one area that worried Tolbuchin – had Suslov's Grey Eagles managed to stop the Fritzes' advance through the high peaks towards the road network?

A thousand kilometres away from the Hungarian front, Adolf Hitler, still conducting the last of the ill-fated Ardennes Offensive from his Western Battle Headquarters at the Castle of Ziegenberg, was concerned too about the progress of his Armed SS.

Facing *Luftwaffe* Colonel Rudel, whom he had just decorated with the highest German award for bravery, he asked the C.O. of the *Immelmann Battle Wing*: 'Well, what do you think of the situation in Hungary, Rudel?'

The burly dive-bomber pilot, who was still flying missions although he had lost a leg and Hitler had expressly forbidden him to do so, did not pull his punches. Aware that the high-ranking staff officers, even the yellow-faced, trembling Führer himself, did not understand what the true situation on the Eastern Front was, he stared around their faces in the big echoing operations room and told the truth. 'It is bloody awful, mein Führer!'

There was a shocked intake of breath from the servile Marshal Keitel, and Colonel-General Jodl, Hitler's Chief-of-Staff, looked sharply at the angry-faced pilot.

'What do you mean, Rudel?' Hitler broke the shocked silence.

'I mean, mein Führer, that we are doing several things wrong up there, which cannot help but make the offensive end in failure.'

'What can we do about the state of the weather, our transport difficulties and so on?' Keitel snapped angrily, his face suddenly flushing with anger.

Rudel turned on him. 'It has nothing to do with weather, transport and such things,' he retorted hotly. 'I fly eight hours a day over the Eastern Front on missions and have been doing ever since 1941, Marshal. I know what's going on. I –'

'What is going on?' Hitler interrupted the pilot's angry outburst, his voice still gentle, almost monotonous.

Next to Hitler, Jodl tensed. He knew that voice of old. At any moment the Führer could explode with a fury of awesome power.

Rudel struck the map with his heavy hand. 'The Vértes Range, mein Führer, out of which the *Fourth S S Panzer Corps* is trying to break east. Yet we all know that its advance is slowing down considerably. Why? Because we have lost the element of initial surprise. Now it stands to reason that the Russians will bring up more and more forces to block the exits out of the mountains. Soon our offensive will bog down altogether.' He paused and let his words sink in.

Next to him, Hitler, peering at the map through his nickel-framed spectacles remained silent.

'So what do we do?' Rudel snorted. 'We batter our heads at a closed door, only to get them beaten bloody. We keep attacking and attacking to no purpose whatsoever.'

'Well, what do you suggest we do, Rudel?' Jodl asked in the arrogant manner of a trained staff officer who had worn the purple leaves of a General Staff member, when this upstart from the *Luftwaffe* was still learning to fly his first glider.

'Roll with the punch, as a boxer does,' Rudel answered without hesitation.

'Explain?' Hitler snapped, his voice normal now, tense and eager.

'Pull the *Fourth SS Corps* out of the mountains, leaving the infantry behind to tie down the Russians, and put them into the battle for Budapest at another spot.'

'Where?'

'Here.' Rudel stabbed the map south of Budapest. 'Here, beyond the Lake[1]. Its first objective should be the Danube south of the capital, say, at Dunapentele. From there, your SS boys could fight due north right into Budapest, taking the Russians by surprise.'

The assembled staff officers listened to the airman's performance with dismay. Yet they knew that his suggestions were influencing Hitler, who despised the General Staff officers and only listened to their advice when he was forced to by some defeat or impending defeat. More often than not he would make his decisions on the basis of his famous 'intuition' or the advice of some 'frontline swine' such as Rudel.

---

1. Lake Balaton.

'But how would we break off the action without the Bolsheviks becoming suspicious, Rudel?' Hitler asked after a moment, his face thoughtful.

'Mein Führer,' the pilot answered. 'I am just a simple soldier, who knows little of higher strategy as these gentlemen do,' he waved his hand at the assembled staff. Jodl's pale, wizened face grew even paler. One day, Rudel, he promised himself, I'll make you pay for that.

'In the days when we flew Stukas, the lead plane would come roaring down out of the sky, sirens howling, machine guns chattering, making the gunners below believe he was going to fall right on top of them, forcing them to concentrate all their fire on him. Meanwhile the rest of the squadron would sneak in at another level and bomb hell out of the real target. A simple feint like that is what you need in those hills, mein Führer. Some device to encourage the enemy to believe that you are still attacking with your armour, while in reality you are withdrawing it to launch a surprise attack on a completely different front, a good fifty kilometres away.'

For what seemed a very long time, Hitler did not respond to Rudel's words. Instead he stared intently at the big table map, as if he could see things there that no one else could. 'A feint,' he said, breaking his long silence. 'That is what you mean, Rudel?'

'Yes.'

'But how and where?'

Jodl intervened: '*SS Regiment Europa*, mein Führer, presently battling its way through the mountains, and apparently to no purpose,' he sneered at Rudel, 'if we are to accept Rudel's suggestion.'

'But not my SS!' Hitler objected.

'Why not, sir?' Jodl answered easily. 'They are beyond recall now and would play no significant role if we were to withdraw the *Viking* and the *Death's Head*, save one. If they were allowed to believe they were spearheading the main drive for Budapest, they might well fool the Russians that we were still pressing ahead with the original plan.'

Hitler looked at his cunning-eyed Chief of Staff. 'But that is a monstrous suggestion, Jodl!' he gasped. 'It. would mean sacrificing many hundreds of brave young men purposelessly.'

'Not purposelessly, sir. If they succeeded in fooling the Russians they would not have died in vain. Besides,' he added as a sudden, malicious afterthought, 'we could give them Rudel's *Immelmann Battle Wing* as air support.' He smiled maliciously in the direction of the most decorated man in the German Forces.

'But we can't fly at those heights –' Rudel began, angrily.

Hitler held up a soft, flabby hand for silence. 'One moment Rudel, while I think about this matter.'

Utter silence descended upon the big room, as Hitler limped to the window and stared out at the bleak, snow-bound landscape. The men of the Armed SS were his Imperial Guard, who had fought and died for him in their hundreds, their thousands, their hundred-thousands on every battlefront. There was no loyalty left in the Army anymore as the Wehrmacht's assassination attempt had proved. But the SS – *his SS* – were they not 'loyal to the death', as their proud motto proclaimed? Could he willingly sacrifice some two thousand bold young men, who believed in him implicitly, for the sake of a tactical manoeuvre?

Even as he turned to face his waiting staff and Rudel again, he already knew that he must.

'Gentlemen,' he announced deliberately, trying to prevent his lips from trembling as they were wont to do since the bomb explosion in his East Prussian HQ that July, 'I have made my decision. I have decided to break off the offensive of the *Fourth SS Panzer Corps*! It will attack again from the south-west, once it has successfully regrouped near Lake Balaton.' Hitler hesitated and directed his yellow, rheumy old eyes at the floor, as if suddenly ashamed. '*SS Regiment Europa will continue its attack in the direction of Budapest.*'

Europa's fate had been sealed.

TWO

The Frenchmen, volunteers all, burst from their cover, heads bent behind the white rain of tracer, doubling towards the dark, unseen peak.

The Russians had not been sleeping after all. Violet light crackled all along their perimeter. Red and green enemy tracer began to cut the air. Behind the French the Cheeseheads intensified their fire, pouring the glowing 20mm shells at a rate of eight hundred a minute at the top of the mountain.

Encouraged by the elan of the French volunteers, Habicht played his next card. Under the covering fire of the flak wagon, another halftrack nosed its snout into the wrecked halftrack which blocked the road and thrust it to one side. Next moment it was rattling towards the peak, its deck crowded with crouching grenadiers.

The Grey Eagles heard rather than saw the danger.

'Flares, in God's name, *flares*!' Suslov yelled urgently.

An instant later two flares burst over the snowfield below, bathing the dark figures struggling valiantly across it in their eerie icy light. Immediately Suslov took in the halftrack rumbling on towards their rear, rattling over the dead, crushing their bodies to bloody pulp.

'Kolchak!' Suslov ordered. 'Stop that vehicle!'

The mortarman rapped out a series of swift orders. The mortar crews worked frantically, ignoring the white hail of death hissing over their heads. '*Ready!*' the first mortar corporal yelled. '*Ready!*' the second followed him a moment later. Kolchak did not hesitate. 'FIRE!' he cried.

The two corporals turned their firing wheels, swinging their heads to one side as the mortars spoke. The first bombs hissed clumsily into the sky.

Suslov's gaze did not leave the dark black shape of the half track, illuminated in the dying flares like some predatory, primeval monster, seeking its prey. The mortars were his only heavy weapon; if they couldn't stop the halftrack its cargo of infantrymen could be delivered right in front of his positions.

But Kolchak was as accurate as ever. The second and third bombs landed right on the open deck of the halftrack. There was a blinding flash of bright white light. Dark shapes whirling and turning in the air against its glare were flung in all directions. Next moment the vehicle's punctured fuel tank exploded, sending a stream of burning red across the snow. Here and there a survivor, already a blazing torch, threw himself vainly into the snow, trying to extinguish the flames which were consuming him alive.

The sight of the burning halftrack took the heart out of the Frenchmen. They broke and ran, streaming back the way they had come, perfect targets against the red glare.

The Grey Eagles rose to their feet, regardless of the 20mm shells still peppering the peak of the mountain, and poured cruel automatic fire into their backs.

The first attack on Grey Eagle Mountain had been repulsed.

'*Damn, damn, damn!* Habicht cursed, striking the metal of the nearest half track with his fist.

Kreuz looked anxiously at Habicht's face – still peppered with the black dried blood of the untreated shrapnel wounds. They could neither go forward nor back. They were trapped on the top of this damn mountain.

'If I could only get the *Royal Tigers* up,' Habicht groaned. 'I'd blast them out of their damn holes like the rats they are!'

'Impossible on this road, *Obersturmbanführer*,' Kreuz said pointedly. 'The outer verge wouldn't support their weight and we can't simply toss the halftracks over the side to make room for them.'

'Of course, of course,' Habicht snarled. 'I know that.' Raising his night glasses, he stared at the stark outline of the peak ahead, as silent now as if it were deserted. 'A frontal attack is out of the question,' he commented to Kreuz.

He swung his glasses to both sides of the peak. 'The flanks are just as bad, even if we could get into position there without their spotting us first.' He raised the glasses and focused them on the sheer rock wall behind the Russian position. His trained Alpinist's eye told him at once that they did not have a hope in hell of getting down there. Yet all the same – he lowered his glasses thoughtfully and turned to Schulze. 'Sarnt-Major.'

'Sir?'

'What would you say off-hand those two automatic rifle cannon might weigh?'

Schulze knew the Hawk meant the two recoilless rifles, Germany's latest secret weapon.

'Fifty kilos or thereabouts, sir,' he said hesitantly.

The Hawk mused, 'A lot of weight to be carried by one man.' He looked at Schulze and the big NCO could see his teeth gleam in a parody of a smile. 'But not if he's as big as you, Schulze, eh?'

'Jesus,' Schulze cursed to himself, 'This is where I crap in my pants!'

Habicht raised his hand as a signal to halt. Schulze with the recoilless rifle strapped to his back and the four big Cheeseheads, laden with shells, flopped into the snow gratefully. They had run the gauntlet of the Russian positions without being spotted, and now they were on the peak, behind the Russians, ready to begin the impossible mission which the Hawk had dreamed up for them.

Close-up the rock face did not look as bad as he had anticipated. The wail sloped at about sixty degrees and was ribbed and terraced pretty fully. There would be plenty of hand- and foot-holds.

Carefully he searched its surface for a convenient ledge: not too high, broad enough to support them and at the same time allow them to see the Reds' positions. Then he spotted it. He focused his glasses on the fault a couple of hundred metres above their heads.

It was broad enough, that was certain, and he was pretty sure that the inky-black darkness of the fold beyond it indicated that there was a deep narrow gully there, which might well overlook the Red positions.

He turned round and looked down at the men on the ground.

'Now listen to me,' he said softly and simply. 'Everybody is frightened on mountains. But the main thing is to keep your head. Once you panic, you are finished. Do you understand that?' He looked directly at the four Dutch volunteers.

'Now you must rely on my judgement implicitly. Where I put my feet – I shall go first – you will put yours. There – and no other place. Clear?'

They nodded their understanding.

'Fine. Our objective is there, that ridge at about ten o'clock.'

Schulze looked up the mountain, following the direction indicated by the Hawk's outstretched arm. 'Oh, Christ!' he exclaimed, 'That's halfway to heaven, that bastard is.'

Habicht chuckled. 'It's not as bad as it looks, Schulze. Believe me.'

Reluctantly the men began to trail through the deep snow in single file behind the Hawk, plodding through its virgin surface like convicted criminals, condemned to a nameless fate.

It was a beautiful winter dawn in the high mountains, the sky above a hard glittering blue and the mountains gleaming an eye-blinking perfect white.

But the Commander of the Grey Eagles had no eyes for the beauty of the morning. His gaze was fixed on the dead littering the snowfield and the burnt-out wreck of the halftrack. What were the SS up to?

He bit his lip and wondered. Would they whistle up their planes? Was that what they were waiting for – air support before they began another attack? Suddenly Major Suslov was strangely uneasy. Turning round he blew his whistle three times to sound the alarm. The men not on stand-to sprang to their feet at once, as if they had not been really sleeping, and grabbed their weapons. Those on stand-to peered alertly from their weapon pits, waiting for orders.

Swiftly Suslov rapped out a stream of commands, putting his Grey Eagles on immediate alert. Veterans that they were, they carried out his orders at once, the new air lookouts seizing binoculars and beginning to search the quarter of the sky allotted to them, while the rest started to hack even deeper holes in the snow for when the German bombers came. But none of them had eyes for the sheer rockface behind their position. There could be no danger from that particular quarter.

After two abortive attempts, Habicht had found what he sought. A sloping ledge took him to a crack and on to a snow-covered platform, perhaps some two hundred metres to the right of the ledge on which he wanted to position the recoilless rifle. It had taken him a good hour of threatening, cajoling, persuading, encouraging to get his men to make it, but in the end he had managed it. Now breathless and obviously not daring to look down at the giddy spectacle of what lay below them, they were ready to attempt the traverse of the rock face to the ledge.

He smiled at them coldly. 'I think we'd better get started now,' he said, 'before you gentlemen take root here.' They were not amused, he could see that. Their eyes, even those of the big NCO, were round and wide with fear like those of sheep, scenting the freshly shed blood and knowing that soon it would be their turn to enter the slaughterhouse.

They began to move across the gleaming face of the mountain towards their objective, sweating profusely in spite of the biting cold and travelling with incredible slowness, but moving all the same.

Habicht led them to a crack. It ran slantwise up a perpendicular rock. He knew it would be easier for them than any other hold. It was not too bad at first, then his foot jammed. Below they halted bewildered by his suddenly frantic struggles to free his foot, but their red, strained faces still showing an almost pathetic belief in his ability to get them to their objective.

Habicht calmed himself. He paused for a moment, forcing himself to be calm, the sweat streaming down and blinding him, his muscles screaming with pain. Gently he tugged at his foot and worked it free. 'Watch that hole,' he called down, controlling his voice with his iron will.

Bringing up the rear with the fifty kilo gun barrel strapped to his shoulders, Schulze was no longer afraid; he was too exhausted to register positive emotion. All his efforts were directed to getting to the ledge which seemed so impossibly far away and slumping down in the snow to rest. The strain was tremendous even for his huge powerful body as the murderous weight of the gun tried to pluck him backwards into the abyss. The sweat streaming down his face, his eyes bulging wildly from his crimson features, he clambered upwards.

And then finally, after what seemed an age, they had made it and were flinging themselves face-downwards on the snow-covered ledge, choking violently for breath. Habicht looked down at them for a moment before crawling carefully to the narrow gully beyond the ledge and peering through it.

He had been right. The Red positions were set out exactly below him at some two hundred metres distance. He could see their every detail – the weapon pits, the snow walls, which sheltered their gunners, the little mortar pit, even the red flag fluttering bravely in the centre of their perimeter.

He had them completely at his mercy. Suddenly *Obersturmbanführer* Otto Habicht chuckled. It was an unearthly sound.

THREE

The flare hissed into the still morning air like a bird of prey. Down below the startled Russians stared up at the green ball of light descending on their perimeter, staining the snow a sickly hue. Gradually the flare came to rest and died a slow, hissing death in the snow.

Everywhere Suslov's Grey Eagles clutched their weapons and stared to their front. The Major, upright next to his command post, machine pistol in hand, was as tense and uneasy as his men. What the hell was going on?

Suslov darted through the scuffed snow and focused his glasses on the bend from which the Fritzes must surely come. There was no sign of activity. One thing he noticed, however. The campfires had gone out. Did that signify the Fritzes were going to attack? Or were they perhaps withdrawing, realizing that it would be impossible to pass his position. His heart leapt with sudden joy. He had stopped the Fritz drive through the mountains with only a handful of casualties – the men lost in the crashed glider. He swung round to his expectant men and opened his mouth to pass on the news. But no words emerged.

For in that same moment, two things happened. Down below engines roared into life, among them the massive rumble of tanks. A second later there was a sharp crack high above his head. He glanced upwards in alarm. Just in time to catch the stab of scarlet flame burning across the snow.

'*Alarm!*' he cried at the top of his voice. '*Stand by everywhere! Mortars?*' – his words were drowned by the crash of a medium sized shell bursting right into the centre of the perimeter and exploding with a hellish roar. The Fritzes had some how managed to get a gun on the height above them! In that same moment, the first halftrack burst round the bend and into the open.

Schulze, crouched behind the long recoilless rifle took careful aim, just as the first halftrack came rattling up the mountain road. Controlling his breathing, he squeezed the trigger gently. The gun thudded against his shoulder. Hot blast swept backwards and the dark flash of the shell whizzed from the muzzle of the strange gun. The shell exploded right in the middle of the Russians manning the furthest mortar. They flew apart, as if punched into the air by some gigantic fist.

'Excellent, Schulze!' Habicht cried exuberantly and ducked as the first enraged burst of Russian machine-gun fire came zipping in their direction.

'Load!' Schulze bellowed. 'Come on you big Cheesehead, move it!'

'*In!*' the, big flaxen-headed Hollander yelled and thrust the shell home.

Schulze took aim again. He pressed the trigger. The gun cracked once more and Schulze cried, 'Now try that one for size, you Popov pigs!'

Suslov fought his panic. If his Eagles could only stop one of the vehicles now emerging from cover, they could still block the way over the pass. 'Kolchak!' he bellowed over the roar of the escaping German halftracks and the firing of the gun on the heights above them. 'Knock me out one of those damn Fritzes. QUICK!'

Suslov left him to it. He grabbed a rifle. 'Boris, get some grenades – from that box there.'

'Smoke?'

'Yes,' Suslov said impatiently, fitting the special grenade-launching device to the rifle. Finished, he kicked the nearest machine-gunner in the ribs. 'You, swing round and give us covering fire up there.'

'But you can't get up there, Major,' Boris protested, ducking smartly as another shell slammed home into the perimeter.

'I know. But at least I can blind the swine, while Kolchak does his job. Come on.'

Together the two of them doubled to the rear of the perimeter, while behind them the machine-gunner opened up, sending a stream of white and red tracer towards the narrow gap high up on the glittering rock face from which the gunfire was coming. They flung themselves into the snow at the base of the rockwall. Frantically Suslov fitted one of the smoke grenades to the top of the long clumsy rifle. He held it upright, pointing straight up at the gorge and fired.

It was an unlucky shot. The grenade struck the rockwall and went ricocheting off like a crazy bird. Suslov muttered a gross obscenity. A heavy stick grenade came whirling down towards them. They ducked as it exploded harmlessly a dozen metres away, showering them with snow. Wildly Suslov raised the rifle knowing that the Fritzes' aim might well be more accurate next time. He fired. This time the dark ball of the grenade sailed right into the entrance of the gully. For a moment nothing happened, then Suslov heard the ping and crack of the grenade exploding. In a flash, thick white smoke started to emerge from the gully.

Ignoring the wild burst of fire from above, Suslov fired grenade after grenade at the opening, as swiftly as Boris could hand them to him knowing now he was effectively masking the Fritz gun and giving Kolchak the time he needed to knock out a halftrack.

Kolchak was ready. He glanced at the level on the big mortar and was satisfied. Below the mountain road was black with the fleeing men. Kolchak raised his arm and then brought it down sharply. 'FIRE!' he bellowed.

The sheet of scarlet flame spewed the dark deadly bomb from the mortar's muzzle. Clumsily it waggled through the air, gaining height by the second until suddenly it seemed to stop, before falling towards the road at a speed, trailing its obscene, stomach churning howl behind it.

Kolchak watched spell-bound as it fell directly in the centre of the line of Fritz halftracks. One of them trembled violently, as if it had been struck by a sudden great wind. The next moment it came to an abrupt stop, thick smoke pouring from its shattered engine, while men sprang frantically over the side before the halftrack caught fire. Behind it the rest of the column around to a halt.

'We've done it, boys!' Kolchak cried, flinging up his arms with joy. 'We've shown the Fritz –'

The words died on his lips. A monstrous shadow lay across the snow at the tail of the stalled convoy.

'A *Royal Tiger*,' Kolchak breathed in horror, as the hooded gun started to swing round slowly in their direction.

'Piss on it!' Schulze cried frantically, trying to control his choking breath. 'Quick!'

The Dutchman ripped open his flies and choking and coughing, the tears streaming down his face with the smoke, he urinated on the dirty handkerchief tendered him. Schulze did not hesitate. He bound the disgusting rag around his mouth. 'Well, don't stand there like a fart in a trance, you stupid Cheesehead. Do the same!' Schulze ordered. 'And bring me some more ammo.'

He dropped onto his belly and crawling through the smoke advanced to the edge of the sheer drop. Ignoring the ricochets and the vicious crack of rifle grenades exploding all around him, he drew his last grenade. Narrowing his eyes against the ever thickening smoke which had blinded the gun, he pulled the china pin at its base and lobbed it over the edge of the rock wall and ducked.

The stick grenade exploded directly below the two Russians.

The snow erupted and obscured them in a wild whirling white storm for a brief moment. When it had cleared, one of them lay sprawled in the snow, his head blown away while the other, helmetless, his clothes ripped by shrapnel and blast, was pelting across the snow the way he had come.

'You'll get a medal for that,' the Hawk's voice cut into Schulze's consciousness. 'I'll see that you do, Schulze when this business is over.'

'Got a whole drawer full of them, Colonel,' Schulze answered. He doubled back to his gun, while the Hawk chopped at the smoke and tried to clear it so that the big NCO could start firing again.

But there was no need for Schulze's recoilless rifle now. In the same moment that Suslov, his face begrimed and smeared with Boris's blood, flung himself headlong into the snow, just behind Kolchak's mortar pit, there was a tremendous roar. It tore the air apart as if in eternal anguish. Even as it engulfed Suslov, wreathing him in its awesome, hot, choking, deafening fury, he knew with a sense of despair what it was. The Fritzes had managed to bring one of the 90mm cannons of their tanks into action. Next moment, the shell exploded right in the centre of Kolchak's mortar pit, one hundred pounds of high explosive, packed in high grade Krupp steel, tearing, ripping, gouging, hacking all in front of it, leaving the pit a smoking horror of mangled, limbless bodies swimming in their own thick, hot blood.

Suslov struggled to his feet. Right at the bend the hooded gun was preparing to fire again. Hurriedly he turned to his terrified radio operator. 'Sergei, tell HQ we can't hold them. We'll have to give up the mountain. Quick!'

'In clear?'

'In clear. No time for code now.' He cringed instinctively as the 90mm cannon spoke again with a mighty roar and the H.E. shell zipped flat across the snowfield with the sound of a huge piece of canvas being ripped apart by a pair of gigantic hands. It exploded in a monstrous burst of crimson flame on the Eagles' perimeter, scything down a good dozen of his men.

The radio operator's finger flew up and down on the key. The man was terrified, veteran that he was, Suslov could see that. But then they all were, himself included. There was no protection against that great gun; even if they dug themselves down as far as hell, it would find them.

'Finished, Comrade Commander,' the radio operator cried over the hellish racket, his voice almost hysterical.

'Sign off!' Suslov yelled. 'We're moving out. Our position here is untenable.'

He blew three shrill blasts on his whistle. The Eagles reacted automatically. They knew the drill well enough. As the German gun fired yet again, every second man left his foxhole and started to retreat to the centre of the perimeter. 'Down the slope to the right,' Suslov commanded, standing proud and erect as was expected of an officer whom Stalin himself had called the 'boldest of the bold'.

The men ran for the cover of the eastern, slope, grateful to be allowed to escape the terrible fury of that murderous gun. Suslov blew his whistle again – twice this time. As the great gun thundered, as if enraged that its chosen victims might yet escape, the last defenders of the perimeter ran out of their foxholes and followed in the direction of the others.

Suslov glanced at his radio operator. 'Pack up and run after them,' he ordered. 'We're finished here now.'

Major Suslov took, one last look at the bodies of his dead littering the perimeter and saluted. Grabbing the shell-torn flag, he turned and began running after the radio operator.

The Battle of Grey Eagle Mountain was over. The way to Budapest was open again.

SECTION FOUR:

BREAKTHROUGH

ONE

'Flight leader here,' Rudel pressed the throatmike, 'are you reading me?'

'I read you...I read you.' The wingmen's answers came back in a quick, metallic blur of words. Colonel Rudel was a strict disciplinarian. In the *Immelmann Battle Wing*, he did not tolerate the easy-going, happy-go-lucky behaviour common to other *Luftwaffe* wings. Rudel believed that one remained alive in combat by minute planning and strict unquestioning discipline.

'Close up...close up...now,' Rudel commanded and eased the throttle of his twin-engined Me 262 jet back slightly.

The two wingmen responded at once. Satisfied he jerked his thumb downwards. They both nodded their understanding. At 550 kilometres an hour, they hurtled out of the sky towards the ground and levelled out at 300 metres.

Now they were roaring along above the mountain road, Rudel leading the flight, while the two wingmen searched the ground for the missing SS regiment.

Rudel did not like the assignment his Wing had drawn one bit. Flying in the mountains in this kind of weather was decidedly dangerous, especially with the raw pilots who made up most of his Wing these days – the veterans had been shot down years before. All the same, he realized that the missing SS regiment's new role was indirectly due to his suggestion. He had a duty to help them the best he could. Besides, he told himself, with a bit of luck and his help, the SS might just win through.

'Colonel Rudel…Colonel Rudel,' a voice filled his ear phones abruptly.

He squeezed the throatmike. 'Yes?'

'To port, sir, looks like a wrecked halftrack.'

Rudel saw it immediately. A burnt-out halftrack, abandoned in a patch of scorched snow, with dark shapes littering the area around it, which he knew were dead men. 'One of ours,' he said over the intercom. 'It's them all right.' They flashed on, the bright white light of the mountain sun gleaming off their canopies as they swung due east, dragging their monstrous black shadows across the snow behind them. To his front Rudel spotted a long line of black dots, moving across the snow at a snail's pace.

'Watch out for flak!' he warned the other two. 'Going down now!'

As one, their wings not more than twenty metres apart; the three planes roared down low, coming in out of the sun to the rear of the convoy to blind their flak gunners. But there was no need for this precaution. Every second vehicle had the swastika recognition flag draped over its bonnet, and the white faces looking up at them were smiling; men were waving their hands in greeting. They had found *SS Regiment Europa*. As the lead halftrack drew away beneath them, Colonel Rudel waggled the wings of the jet in acknowledgement and swept on down the road to check out the opposition undoubtedly awaiting the condemned Regiment.

An enormous black shadow shot over the road. The Guards Cavalry troopers cast frightened eyes upwards, as the second jet came screaming in, its cannon chattering. They scattered wildly, horses snorting wide-nostrilled with fear.

Rudel came in for his run. He glanced in his mirror. That last glance had saved his life many a time in the last years, but there was no Russian fighter on his tail. The roadblock had no air cover. He eased the stick back. The engine noise died to a whisper. The jet seemed to drop like a stone. The stall warning buzzers started screaming. Rudel ignored them, as he continued with the manoeuvre for which he was famous throughout the *Luftwaffe*. The ground was only fifty metres below him now. He could make out the fleeing Russians quite distinctly.

The scream of the warning buzzers had reached a peak. If he did not react soon, the plane would crash. He pressed the firing button. The cannon sputtered. Twenty millimetre shells hissed at the Russians like angry red hornets. Men fell everywhere. A horse had its hind legs blown off, but tried to struggle on over the snow, dragging its intestines behind it like an obscene grey-green snake.

Rudel caught the jet just in time. He was thrust back hard against his seat, as both engines regained full thrust, and zoomed high into the sky, leaving his two wingmen the job of demolishing the hastily erected road block with their cannon. His message was simple. 'Rudel to *Europa*. Road out of the mountains clear now. Courtesy *Immelmann Battle Wing*. Good luck!'

Half an hour later, the advance party of *SS Regiment Europa* came to a halt at the site of the massacre, and the two vehicles rolled to a stop. Cautiously Habicht and Schulze, followed by the Chink and a couple of other troopers, advanced on the shattered mess up the road. But there was no need for their caution. The men lying everywhere in the shell-pitted snow were dead.

Habicht thrust his pistol back in its holster and placing his leather map case on the rump of a dead horse, spread his map, while behind him the Chink began to loot the bodies, quietly but efficiently. Habicht looked up at Schulze: 'Sergeant-Major, I want you to listen carefully. In perhaps another kilometre or so, we shall be out of the mountains and joining the main road network to Budapest, which is exactly twenty kilometres away from that junction. A mere twenty kilometres, imagine that.' He looked at Schulze almost proudly.

Schulze's broad red face remained expressionless, not revealing his misgivings about the great offensive, which had been growing throughout the morning.

'Now we know that the bulk of the Red forces are located in front of the Bickse and Zsambek positions where the *Viking* and the *Death's Head* are attempting to make their main break-outs. We can assume that the main east-west axis from Budapest should be packed with second-line troops, the rear echelon and the like. With the men at our disposal we cannot cope with that kind of thing. Besides I don't want to get involved in unnecessary minor action. So we must find another road to Budapest.

'A secondary road – something of that kind – which would be big enough to take the *Royal Tigers*, possibly running parallel but to the south of the main axis. Now once the regiment hits the main road here, I cannot afford to hesitate. Hesitation could well mean we could become bogged down in some Red counter-attack. When we arrive there, I want to be across that main road and on my secondary road immediately.'

Schulze knew he was a fool even as he posed the question. 'But how will you know which secondary road to choose, sir?'

Habicht smiled at him but there was no answering warmth in that glacial-grey eye of his. 'You will tell me, Schulze. You are the only man capable of it.'

'You mean, sir, you want me to carry out a forward recce and radio back the details of the way ahead to the rest of the Regiment – all the way to Budapest? He looked at the Hawk aghast. '*For twenty kilometres behind the Popov lines?*'

Habicht ignored the shocked look on the NCO's face. 'Yes. That little *Hiwi* driver of yours speaks fluent Russian and I believe I have a ploy which will conceal you from discovery.' He extended his one arm at the dead Russians lying everywhere in the bloody, scuffed snow. 'You could wear Russian uniform – you and your *Hiwi*.' He smiled at Schulze, as if it were the most obvious thing to do in the world.

'But, sir,' Schulze said, 'may I point out to you that the Popov shoot people who wear their uniform. In their naïve manner they seem to think that they are spies.'

'Yes, I suppose they do,' Habicht answered easily. 'But that, I'm afraid, is a chance you will have to take.'

Schulze and Chink had just completed their transformation into Russian soldiers of the Guards Cavalry Division when the shooting began.

The Hawk had intended to use the prisoners taken on the mountain as a human protective screen to walk in front of the column and force whoever was holding the expected barrier on the road to surrender or shoot their own comrades. But Rudel had taken care of that particular problem for him. Now he had no need of the Grey Eagles, and with his habitual desire to rid the world of as many Russians as possible before he died, he had them lined up in the snow and mown down by machine-gun.

Chink watched with a look of disapproval on his yellow face. 'Chink think no good,' he mumbled. 'No shoot prisoners in Red Army – well not much.'

Schulze looked at the fat little *Hiwi*. 'Better dead than red, Chink,' he said without too much conviction, adjusting the collar of his newly acquired overcoat.

'No good – very bad,' the Chink persisted.

Gloomily he stamped towards the jeep, its bonnet camouflaged with netting to hide the telltale swastika, while Schulze went across to take leave from Habicht. The Hawk was in one of his heady, electric moods. He took his gaze from where the two Frenchmen were draping the *Europa* across the dead Russians' chests, as was the Regiment's practice and said joyously. 'Well, Schulze, all ready to go?'

'Yessir.'

'You know just how important the mission I've given you is. Find me that road to Budapest and you can have anything that it is my power to give you.'

'I'll do my best, sir.'

'I know you will, Schulze.'

The big NCO strode back to the jeep, where the Chink was already gunning the motor noisily, as if he could not wait to get away from the grim sight of the murdered paratroopers. A moment later they were on their way.

Up on the heights, Major Suslov lowered his binoculars slowly, the tears streaming unrestrained down his handsome face. He had seen enough. His brave Eagles had been slaughtered in cold blood by the Fritz swine.

While the survivors of the battle stared at him in awed silence, Major Suslov wiped the tears from his eyes and said in a strained voice, full of anger and anguish. 'Grey Eagles, I swear to you I will kill every one of the fascist pigs for what they have done to our comrades down there. I swear!' He raised his right hand into the air, as if he were pledging a solemn oath.

And then the German jets were coming again, winging low over the snow at a tremendous speed as part of the cover supplied by *Immelmann Battle Wing* and the Grey Eagles were scattering wildly for the safety of the nearest fir wood.

TWO

On the fifth day of the surprise German offensive, which now seemed to be slackening off in the Vértes Mountains, Marshal Tolbuchin's troops assaulted and captured the most important height on the western bank of the Danube: Gellert Hill. Rising steeply to a height of nearly 250 metres, it dominated the Buda half of Budapest, which was held by Colonel Doerner's Germans and their still loyal Hungarian allies under the command of Colonel-General Ivan von Hindy, some 70,000 men in all.

As soon as the news came in that the assault of his picked storm troops had been successful, Tolbuchin ordered the General commanding the attack on the remaining half of the city to rush his artillery up the Gellert Hill and begin a systematic destruction of Buda. 'Smoke the rats out,' he commanded, 'and then send in your tanks to finish the job off. I want Buda captured without delay.'

The local commander obeyed with alacrity. Every gun available was rushed up the height to commence the destruction of Buda, which was cut off from Pest by the destruction of the eight bridges spanning the Danube. Hour after hour they poured their fire into the old town around the Castle Hill.

The German–Hungarian resistance along the Danube line began to weaken. One by one their defence posts crumbled under the massive bombardment. The first T-34s started to cross the Danube and attempted to penetrate deeper into Buda, flight after flight of rockets covering their progress across the burning water.

The defenders retreated, blocking key intersections with over-turned trams, interlaced with timbers and torn-up tramlines. They had few anti-tank weapons but plenty of ingenuity. They greased the old cobbled streets with engine grease, waste oil and industrial liquid soap. When the T-34s hit the greased patches, they slid and skidded violently, their drivers swiftly losing control, making themselves easy targets for the volunteers with their Molotov cocktails.

Similarly hollows or depressions in the well-worn streets were filled with petrol and when the T-34s rattled through what they took to be water, a soldier hidden in a doorway would fling a phosphorous grenade into the petrol, swamping the tank in a sudden awesome blaze.

Brown earthenware plates of the kind used by poorer Magyar families were strung across the roads so that they could be easily seen and taken for a daisy chain of mines by the Soviet tank crews. Fearful of rolling over them, the tankers would back down the narrow streets to run right into a chain of hand grenades suddenly pulled into their blinded rear. Trams, packed with high explosives, were set hurtling down the steep narrow streets of the Castle Hill district to ram the invaders. High tension wires were dropped upon them as they passed by, electrocuting their crews. Empty oxygen cylinders were rolled under their tracks as they ground their way round the treacherous bends of the narrow, steeply inclined streets sending the great machines crashing against the buildings.

But still they pressed on, followed by assault squads of picked infantry, who were armed with flame-throwers and burnt their way systematically from house to house and from street to street with their terrible weapons, leaving behind them a fearsome smoking wreckage of crashed trams, ruined houses, wrecked tanks.

Siberian infantry followed and died in the German fire by their hundreds. The fact they were simply cannonfodder to be used up before Tolbuchin sent in his élite Guards did not seem to perturb them. They died in the same manner as they raped the scream-ing Hungarian housewives and their daughters, impassively and without comment.

As night fell on that fifth day, the Siberians broke into the German telephone HQ, manned by a handful of middle-aged sol-diers and a hundred or more 'field mattresses', as the German sol-dier called their female auxiliaries contemptuously. The drunken Siberians threw their lives away foolishly, forcing the German soldiers back and back into the telephone building until all of them were dead and the screaming terrified women were theirs. They knew no mercy.

Hidden beneath a dead body, the lesbian supervisor of the exchange, feigning death and looking no different, in her *Wehrmacht* trousers and cropped hair, than the dead soldiers all around her, took in the terrible mass rape. She watched how three of them raped little Ingrid, the virgin for whom she had lusted herself; how they ripped the clothes off a screaming 'Fat Erna' whose enormous breasts fell down to her bulging stomach when they cut away her bra; how they fought each other with knives and bayonets to enjoy the favours of 'Granny', the white-haired, eldest member of the troop, because they believed that an old woman had a special magic.

And before she fainted with revulsion, she saw how one of them, enraged beyond measure by the fiery resistance of Eva, the one-time German Maiden leader, smashed an axe against her face, causing a horrific gaping wound. When in his drunken state he could not make love to her bleeding unconscious body, he thrust the axe handle up between her thighs and raising his booted foot, gave it a vicious kick which sent it deep into her cruelly tortured body, the hot blood seeping out from between her legs in a scarlet stream.

When the middle-aged Doerner heard of these outrages, he ordered the immediate evacuation of the remaining auxiliaries to the suburbs where *SS Obergruppenführer* von Pfeffer Wildenbruch held out with his two SS cavalry divisions. He spoke on the telephone to Colonel-General von Hindy, Commander of the 1st Hungarian Corps, and asked him to counter-attack immediately with his two weak infantry divisions.

Von Hindy was obviously at the end of his tether, but he was the typical old school K-u-K[1] officer. 'My men are hungry. They have no ammunition to speak of and nothing more than machine guns to ward off the Russian tanks —' he began.

'The situation is desperate, I know,' Doerner exclaimed. 'But I must ask you to do your best.'

Von Hindy did not seem to hear Doerner's words. He continued, 'But we are Hungarians and Hungarians have always been fools about such things. Colonel we shall attack as soon as it grows dark.'

'*Brave* fools,' Doemer said to himself as he put down the phone and began the virtually impossible task of trying to re-establish his crumbling line with the middle-aged policemen who made up his command.

Thus it was that Colonel-General von Hindy's surprise counter-attack into Buda caught Tolbuchin unawares and forced him to withdraw the Guards battalions, which had been dug in behind the main Bickse–Budapest road, to use them against the new threat.

It was into this suddenly open gap that Chink and Sergeant-Major Schulze slipped, as that terrible Saturday finally came to an end.

---

1. Imperial and Royal. Title applied to the old Anglo-Hungarian Army, prior to 1918.

THREE

The jeep rolled cautiously the first village Schulze and Chink had encountered on their reconnaissance drive.

Chink changed down to second, while Schulze, his finger round the trigger of the round-barrelled Russian machine-gun stared at the single storey, tumbledown cottages with their crooked chimneys from which no smoke rose. The place looked empty. But he knew they could not be too careful.

As they entered the little settlement, they soon learned there was nothing to be afraid of. The village was dead – wiped out.

Men – and women, their skirts thrown back obscenely, their legs thrust apart – lay everywhere in the dirty snow. From the black skeletal trees in the village square, naked men hung by their necks, their faces black, their bodies as hard as board. Just outside the church, the village priest was nailed upside down to the big wooden crucifix, his amputated penis thrust in between his gaping lips.

Schulze retched and fought back the bitter bile which threatened to flood his throat. 'Christ almighty Chink, who did this?' he exclaimed.

'The Russians,' a soft voice in German said behind them. The two of them spun round.

A little man, dressed in a brown, overlong leather coat and a fur hat with loose earflaps was standing there.

'Who are you?' Schulze demanded, raising the gun. The little man raised his hands but the smile remained on his cunning face. 'Janosz is the name, sir,' he said. 'Janosz the Pedlar, they call me in these parts.'

Schulze lowered his weapon slowly. 'How do you know we are German?' he asked. The man pointed to the back of the VW jeep. 'German number. SS too. I thought you were the Russians coming back but when I saw that number I came out of my hiding place, knowing that our allies had returned.'

'What happened here?' Schulze asked.

'They were ordered back to the siege of Budapest last night. It annoyed them. The Guards thought they were going to have an easy, safe time here, sitting out the battle. They got drunk. After that their officers couldn't control them.' He extended one dirty hand as if revealing to them some splendid tableau, his wizened cunning face devoid of any emotion. 'You can see the result.'

'You're a Yid,' Chink burst out suddenly, a look of accusation on his yellow face.

'That is correct,' Janosz the Padlar replied impassively.

Schulze was caught off guard for a moment. Was the man off his head, or simply very brave in admitting he was one of the persecuted race? He decided that the Jew was neither; he was cunning. He had revealed himself like this to the two of them delivering his life into their hands, as it were, because he had some plan. 'Now listen Ikey, don't try pulling any Jewboy tricks on me, or I'll dock your prick a lot shorter than the Rabbi ever did! What's yer game?'

The little man smiled slowly. 'Game? No game, honourable sir. Just a little proposition. A matter of business.'

'Business?' Schulze echoed, while Chink's suspicious look was changed to one of guarded interest.

'I have the impression that you gentlemen are on your way to Budapest, perhaps as a forerunner of others.' He shrugged slightly. 'It is no concern of mine. But if you were prepared to take me to the capital, I could ensure you did not bump into any of the enemy on their way.' He looked at the giant NCO out of the corner of his dark smart eyes; as if he felt the German might be scared by the impact of his full gaze.

'But what do you want to go to Budapest for?'

'Sir, I have been wandering these roads now for forty years. I am weary of it. You Germans call the Magyars the "hungry people". I am sick of hungry people too. I think I would like to spend my old age with the Chosen People,' he smiled to himself at the use of the word, 'in Palestine, and for that indulgence I need money. In Budapest in such confusing times as these, there is money to be made – much money. I will obtain some of it.' He said the words as a simple statement of fact, not conjecture.

Schulze stared at the little man thoughtfully. Slowly a plan was beginning to form in the back of his big head – vague and incoherent as yet, but there all the same. 'All right, Ikey, you're on. You can lead us to Budapest.'

Five minutes later Schulze had radioed their position and the map reference of the road they were taking east, and shortly afterwards the three of them set off in the little jeep to the accompaniment of Schulze's: 'A Chink, a Yid and a senior NCO of the Armed SS in a jeep together! *What would the Führer say!*'

The little Jew was true to his word. All that long Sunday, he directed them down little side roads, country tracks, through empty, looted, raped villages, avoiding the Russian mobile patrols time and time again. In the afternoon it started to snow again, thick heavy soft flakes which made the going treacherous. Through the battling windscreen wipers, the silent fir forests on both sides slid past, while Schulze concentrated on driving.

Just as he changed down and prepared to negotiate a steep hill, the little Jew said urgently but without any apparent fear, 'There are Russians up there, Sergeant-Major.'

Automatically Schulze hit the brake and the jeep slithered to a stop, a pillow of snow dropping on the hood from a tree with a plopping crunch. 'Where?'

'On the height.'

Schulze saw them. A long line of cavalry riding noiselessly through the streaming white wall of snow like grey ghosts, heading into the forest.

With tensed breath, they waited till they had ridden past, Schulze ready to slam into reverse. But there was no need; the cavalrymen did not spot them.

'You've got good eyes for a Yid, Ikey!' Schulze said, as he thrust home first and prepared to tackle the hill.

'It is because I have such good eyes that I have survived, dear sir,' the little man answered. 'Yids, as you call us, need good eyes, and a good nose for danger. We die young if we don't have them.'

Just before darkness fell, their luck ran out. They had left the country lanes because of the deeply packed snow and were driving cautiously down a second-class road. By now they were all exhausted; even Schulze's giant frame was tired after a day's driving in those terrible conditions. Perhaps it was for that reason that none of them spotted the big, six-wheeled armoured car with the dull red star on its turret until it was almost too late.

'Russian!' the old man yelled in alarm.

Schulze acted instinctively. As the armoured car came out of its harbour at the side of the road and fired, Schulze swung the wheel desperately to the right and went skidding and bouncing up a narrow trail which led steeply upwards through the close-packed firs. An instant later the 37mm shell exploded in a spurt of angry scarlet on the spot where they had been a moment before.

The four-wheel drive whining in first, Schulze drove the VW jeep up the incline, fighting the terrain, skidding time and time again, and threatening to roll backwards.

'They come other road!' Chink cried, as he caught a glimpse of the big armoured car through a gap in the forest. The armoured car was tearing up the road almost parallel to them. A moment later Schulze swung round a bend and discovered that the two vehicles were on converging paths.

Schulze put his foot to the floor. The VW bowled along, the crossroads only fifty metres away now. The armoured car saw them. Its machine guns chattered. Tracer zipped through the green gloom towards them. Schulze just made the crossroads before the armoured car which swung round and headed after the bouncing, bucking VW. The vehicle's 37mm cracked into action once more. A sudden brown hole appeared in the surface of the snow to their right like the work of some gigantic mole.

The gun fired again. To their left the firs were sheared away and went crashing down in a flurry of snow like matchsticks. They reached another steep slope. To their right the mountainside fell steeply. Now the armoured car's massive horse power began to tell, and it started to gain on them again, its machine guns chattering furiously. Schulze's eyes strained through the flying snow, trying to make out the top of the ascent. If they did not make it soon and swing round the cover of some bend, they would be finished. The armoured car would overtake them. The snow cleared for a moment and Schulze saw with an overwhelming sense of defeat that there was perhaps a quarter of a kilometre of straight road ahead of them to the next bend. They could not make it!

But he had not reckoned with the old Jew. Suddenly he seemed to forget his fear. He thrust his skinny hand through the flap at his side and began undoing the strap which held the spare jerrican of petrol fixed to the side of the VW. Supporting himself in the wildly swaying VW as best he could, he managed it and ripped open the filler cap. The VW was suddenly full of the stink of petrol. He let go of the can. It fell behind them, bouncing and tumbling on the hard-packed snow of their tracks, right into the path of the armoured car. The driver had no time to manoeuvre. Next instant, there was the hollow clang of steel striking steel. What was left of the petrol – perhaps ten or so litres – washed up and covered the whole front of the armoured car's glacis plate.

Abruptly Chink realized what the old man was up to. He did not hesitate, but, plunged his clenched fist through the thin plastic of the rear window, and pulled out a stick grenade. Schulze watched fascinated in the rear view mirror, at the armoured car, dripping petrol, looming ever larger. Then the Russians were close enough. '*Urrah!*' Chink yelled and flung the grenade.

It exploded exactly where he wanted – on the link between the turret and the petrol-soaked glacis plate. The grenade itself did no harm to the hardened steel of the car, but the heat of its explosion ignited the petrol.

In a flash, the whole front of the armoured car was alive with bright red flame, completely blinding the driver. Instinctively he hit the brakes. It was a deadly thing to do on that slope and in that snow. The armoured car skidded crazily to the right. For one long moment it teetered on the edge of the cliff. But there was no holding it now.

As Schulze pressed the brakes gently and brought the VW to a stop, the flaming armoured car went over the side and then tumbled from view. He heard the outcome far below: the long jarring crunch as it hit the first rocks, followed by the brittle shattering of steel as it struck outcrop after outcrop until it came to rest in one great echoing crash at the bottom.

Schulze wiped the mixture of sweat and snow from his broad, scarlet face gratefully and looked down at the little Jew, who was beaming at him. 'You know, Ikey, you saved our bacon just then.'

'We survived,' the little man said easily.

'Here,' Schulze said spontaneously, 'I've got something for you.' He reached inside the Russian greatcoat and tugged out his Knight's Cross of the Iron Cross. 'Stick that round yer skinny Yiddish neck,' Schulze said.

Janosz the Pedlar looked down incredulously at the gleaming black and white decoration now hanging from his neck. Then shaking his old head, he followed the other two back to the bullet-holed jeep.

'*Oi, oi,*' he muttered to himself as he clambered inside again, 'a Yid with the Iron Cross. *Meschugge!*'

Moments later they were on their way towards Budapest.

FOUR

'Otto, we request Otto?' the radio operator's cracked hoarse voice was the only sound in the little stone barn. 'Great Hawk do you read me…we need Otto urgently.'

Habicht, standing next to Kreuz, seemed unconcerned that *Europa* had been unable to raise Division – 'Great Hawk' – all day, and that there was no 'Otto' – fuel – forthcoming. But Kreuz knew that inwardly the C.O. was worried. They had slipped through the Russian lines quite easily, and now they would make their last dash for Budapest. But to what purpose, if there was no Division *Viking* to follow them up?

With a sigh the radio operator took off his sticky headphones and turned to face Habicht, dark violet circles under his blood shot eyes. 'Sir, I don't think I'd raise them if I tried till I was blue in the face. It's almost as if they're not there, sir,' he ended a little desperately.

'Of course Division is there!' Habicht snapped. 'Try again, man!'

Reluctantly the radio operator put on his earphones once more, while Habicht dismissed his young officers.

'What about you, Kreuz?' Habicht asked, when his second- in-command showed no signs of moving.

Major Kreuz had had enough. He was not a professional soldier like Habicht. He had joined the pre-war Berlin *Reitersturm*[1] of the SS because it was the chic thing to do. In this way he had come to the SS and he had fought their battles loyally enough throughout the war. But he had not the self-sacrificing fanaticism of the regular SS officer. Now he wanted to save his skin while there was still time.

'*Obersturmbannführer*, I would like to speak to you – outside.'

Habicht looked at him curiously and nodded agreement. Slowly they walked through the sleeping village, the only sound the crisp slow tread of the sentries on the hard snow. Kreuz stopped and faced his commander.

'Habicht, you must be realistic.'

Habicht looked at the pale, unshaven, self-indulgent face in the cold-blue light of the moon and knew his second-in-command was deathly afraid. 'What do you mean, Major – realistic?'

'About the Division. We couldn't get the Division, because it is simply not there.'

'What do you mean?'

'Look at the horizon, to the west.'

'I see nothing.'

'*Exactly*, Habicht. For the simple reason that the Division has pulled out – isn't that obvious?'

'Impossible,' Habicht snapped icily. 'Absolutely impossible!' In sudden anger Kreuz went the whole way. 'The offensive has failed, I tell you, and we are all risking our necks for nothing.' He stared at the tall C.O., his face flushed with emotion.

'You and your precious neck,' Habicht said contemptuously. 'We are exactly ten kilometres away from Budapest now. So far Schulze has done his job. With the same luck tomorrow, we could well be in the capital by nightfall.'

Kreuz stared at him aghast. 'You're crazy, Habicht! You have lost all contact with reality,' he exploded, knowing now that there was no turning back; he had said it. 'There is no bloody follow-up!

---

1. SS Cavalry Unit.

We will be just joining the rest of the poor bastards trapped there by the Russians.'

'We shall have made history,' Habicht harked, iron in his voice. '*Europa* will have led the first successful German offensive for nearly two years.'

'Do you really think anyone cares? You might want to waste your life, Habicht, but I'm not going to let you waste mine and those of all your young men. I don't suffer from your kind of death wish.'

'What do you mean, Kreuz?'

'I mean that I am going to rouse the officers out of their beds and tell them what the real situation is. I shall recommend to them that the Regiment should withdraw, while there is still time, to our lines at Bickse.'

'That is mutiny!'

'Not when one is led by a maniac. And don't believe you can frighten me with the threat of a court-martial. Germany is falling apart too quickly for that to worry me. You can't stop…'

His voice died in his throat. Habicht was holding a pistol pointed directly at him.

'What the devil, Habicht,' he began, his face suddenly contorted with terror.

He never finished the sentence. The pistol kicked in the Hawk's hand, shattering the silence of the night. Kreuz screamed and flew backwards through the night, the blood seeping through his shattered guts. Calmly Habicht walked over to where he lay in the suddenly darkened snow and placed his pistol against the side of Kreuz's head. His face expressionless, he blew his skull apart.

'Major Kreuz has just met with a fatal accident,' he said to the running sentries, alarmed by the shooting. They stopped short and looked down at the mutilated body, lying crumpled in the ever-growing red star of its own blood, their young eyes wide with shock and bewilderment.

'You'd better throw some snow over him or something,' Habicht said carelessly. 'I wouldn't like the men to see him like that at dawn.'

Up in front, Habicht's oddly assorted reconnaissance team had hit trouble. Just before dusk they had reached the river which formed the Russian second-line around the western suburbs of Budapest. No way across was apparent and to make matters worse, as soon as it had grown really dark, the Russians had switched on huge searchlights, which probed the night with long fingers. They abandoned the jeep, which was too conspicuous, and vanished into the snow-heavy pine forest which lined the western bank of the unknown river.

Now the three of them crawled ever closer to a little ford which the Jew knew of. It, too, was illuminated, but according to Janosz unguarded. Between the trees they could make out the river across which searchlights threw sinister patterns at ten second intervals.

'What do you think, Ikey?'

The little Jew stroked his beard thoughtfully. 'You need me, Sergeant-Major. I need you. You will be able to get through the river and beyond the wire before the searchlights illuminate it again. I am too slow, too old, too frail –'

'Knock it off,' Schulze interrupted him brutally. 'You'll have me breaking down and crying in a minute, you short-cocked kike!'

Janosz continued imperturbably: 'I shall send you, Sergeant-Major to get through the barbed wire, where you will leave our Chinese friend here. Then, you put out those search lights and our friend here will come back and fetch me.'

Schulze looked at him open-mouthed. 'And why,' he asked finally, 'should a senior non-commissioned officer of the Armed SS and his Chink servant come back and collect one scruffy docked-tailed Yid who we don't need any more, eh?'

The Jew smiled, as if at the folly of human understanding. 'But you do need him, Sergeant-Major. My dear German friend, you might just want to come out again,' he hesitated for only a fraction of a second, 'and who will there be to show you the way?'

'You!'

'Exactly.'

Behind them, Chink beamed and said: 'Jew, him pretty smart feller.'

Jonasz the Pedlar allowed himself another smile.

FIVE

Schulze waded cautiously through the shallows hoping the faint hollow boom of the guns at the front would hide the noise. Behind him Chink, laden down with the radio, struggled in the freezingly cold current.

Schulze clambered up the bank and tugged Chink up with one heave of his powerful shoulders.

'Right, you slant-eyed devil, as soon as those twin searchlights have moved on, I'm going to double for the wire. When I'm over it, you should hear a couple of shots. That'll be me knocking out the lamps.' Chink nodded. 'Then you pull your yellow finger out of your yellow arse and run back like hell to fetch the Yid. Don't forget to bring the radio with you when you come over the wire.'

'Chink now savvy.'

'Thank Christ for that,' Schulze said and directed his attention to the twin searchlights. Their beams did not always coordinate but he reckoned he might have fifteen seconds to double the hundred odd metres across the field and fling himself over the wire. It was not enough. Then he spotted a slight hollow runnel which led from the river to within about sixty metres of the wire before it petered out where the ground was completely exposed to the searchlights. There was his chance!

Suddenly he set off, crawling swiftly down the hollow. The twin lights caught him just as he reached the end. He lay stock still, face pressed tight to the cold snow. The yellow reflected light seemed to pin him there for an eternity. All his muscles were drawn painfully tight as he fought against the temptation to break and run before they saw him and the machine-guns tore his body to shreds. But no machine-guns opened up. A moment later the lights passed on and he was up and running madly for the wire.

Legs pumping, arms driving, the snow spurting up around his feet, he flung himself upwards and cleared the fence. His heart pounding furiously, he lay still as the lights swept the ground behind him yet once again, while he remained this time in complete darkness. Now for the second phase!

He could see the operators quite clearly, stark black silhouettes against the white glare of the light. They moved slowly and without much energy, in spite of the cold. There were four of them, but that did not worry Schulze. He could catch them completely unawares.

He glanced briefly at the second light. It was about two hundred metres away and the suspicions of the crew would probably not be aroused after the first one went out until a couple of minutes had elapsed. They must be used to technical flaws in such a climate. If he worked quickly, he could get them both.

He rose to his feet and almost casually began to walk towards the searchlight crew, the hoods in which they were huddled drowning the crisp noise his boots made on the frozen snow.

Schulze was only five metres away when the man next to the steadily throbbing generator spotted him. '*Stoi?*' he demanded, obviously startled.

Schulze did not give him a chance to say any more. He belted him with his 'Hamburg equaliser', the set of brass knuckles he had always taken with him to the Hamburg whorehouses. The man slammed against the side of the mobile generator and slumped limp-headed to the ground, without a sound. Schulze advanced on the other men grouped around the light.

His big right arm reached out of the darkness and grabbed the nearest man, his hand over the man's mouth stifling the instinctive cry of fear. He squeezed – very hard. The man sighed, as if tired and happy to go to sleep. He did. For good. Gently Schulze lowered him to the ground.

Something must have warned the survivors. They swung round and stared aghast at this gigantic shape emerging from the darkness. The nearest man opened his mouth to yell, but Schulze's right boot thudded into his crotch. He went down gurgling vomit. The other man ran. Schulze dived forward. His 'Hamburg equaliser' clubbed down. The Russian jinked and the brutal set of brass knuckles hit him on the shoulder. For a moment the two men wrestled violently in front of the blazing light like actors in a Chinese shadow play, then Schulze's knuckleduster connected. There was a sharp click. The Russian's spine broke. He dropped helplessly to the snow. Schulze did not hesitate. He ground the nail-studded heel of his big jackboot into the helpless man's face and churned it to a bloody lifeless pulp.

Blinded by the glare, Schulze fumbled in the red darkness behind the searchlight to find the switch. He snapped it off and at once the bright light died. Schulze sprinted towards the other one.

He ran until he was about twenty-five metres away from it. In a moment the other crew would swing their own light round to check the trouble. Carefully he raised his Schmeisser and took aim. At that range the long hard burst of fire was deadly accurate. There was a sound of splintering glass, curses, a long drawn-out scream of agony and abruptly the light went out. He had done it!

It was nearly dawn now. The little Jew led them unerringly through the kilometre-wide no-man's land between the Russian and German positions. Across a silent, ice-covered canal. Through a frozen marsh, where the white reeds, heavy with hoar frost, cracked alarmingly when their boots brushed against them.

Between two abandoned and ruined farmhouses, dead pigs lying everywhere like tethered barrage balloons.

Just before six, Janosz stopped them.

'What is it?' Schulze demanded..

'We're there,' the Jew whispered. He pointed with a skinny finger. 'Do you see that little height? It is the first German machine-gun position. It's in what's left of old Ferenc Kobol's barn. I have slept there many a winter's night on my travels.' Janosz smiled warily. 'This is where I leave you. I shall make my own way into Buda from here as I doubt if your fellow countrymen would welcome a Jew with open arms. But when yon need me, Sergeant-Major, you'll find me or someone who'll know where I am in the Kobanyai Street. It's near Burgberg, the Citadel.'

'And who do I ask for – Janosz the Pedlar?'

Suddenly the little man was embarrassed. 'No,' he said hesitantly. 'In Buda, I have another name – Csoki. It means "Little Chocolate Drop". Because that was what I peddled in Buda before the war – chocolate drops.'

Schulze smothered a laugh. 'All right,' he said, eager to be away now, 'I'll come looking for you when the time is ripe, my little Yiddish Chocolate Drop.'

The old man departed in the direction of Buda without further ado, disappearing out of their lives as mysteriously as he had appeared. Schulze and Chink wasted no more time. Hurriedly they made their way to the frontline outpost.

'*Wer da?*' a voice rapped out suddenly, heavy with frightened surprise. '*Halt oder ich schiesse!*'

Slowly Schulze rose from the ground – he knew these trigger-happy young sentries – and lifted his arms into the air. 'Take it easy now,' he said softly. 'You've just been rescued, soldier-boy, by the advance party of *SS Regiment Europa*.'

Two hours later in a brilliantly executed lightning attack, *Obersturmbannführer* Habicht forded the undefended river and with his monstrous *Royal Tigers* in the van, burst a quarter of a kilometre hole in the Russian front line. Taken completely by surprise, the Russian riflemen scrambled out of their holes and fled in terror, leaving the SS Regiment to file through the gap without a single casualty and pass into the lines of the hard-pressed *22nd SS Cavalry Division* to be fêted like heroes. They had reached Budapest at last.

SECTION FIVE:

BATTLE OF BUDAPEST

ONE

At 5a.m. Friday, 18 January 1945, the new attack to break through to Budapest began in a snowstorm. From their new positions around Lake Balaton, the *4th SS Panzer Corps*, with the *3rd Panzer Division* to their right and the *1st Panzer Division* to their left, raced forward to overcome the surprised first-line Russian positions. The plan was for the SS panzer divisions in the middle to make the running, while the two Army panzers on the flanks contained any Russian attempt at a counter-attack. The SS panzers would have as their first objective the ford across the canal at Kaloz, which was the major physical barrier on the way to the River Danube, and their second objective the little town of Dunapentele south of Budapest.

The new plan, the result of Rudel's conference with Hitler, worked like a charm. After a short preliminary artillery bombardment and led by Rudel's *Immelmann Battle Wing*, the *Tigers* and *Panthers* of the *Viking* and the *Death's Head*, followed by waves of panzer grenadiers in halftracks, burst through the Russians and disappeared into the snowstorm before the enemy had realized what had hit them. That first day, the SS panzers, their flanks barely defended by the more hesitant *Wehrmacht* divisions, pushed a wedge thirty kilometres deep into the Russian position.

But in the evening *Viking* ran into serious trouble. The Russians had not only mined the area to their front, they had also introduced a new obstacle – wire charged with high voltage electricity. Even the battle-hardened SS officers hesitated to send their young European volunteers and their German comrades against such defences. The *Viking* attack bogged down. General Gilles, commander of the *Fourth SS Panzer Corps*, made a personal appearance at the Division's Command Post. The elderly, bespectacled, normally good-humoured Corps Commander was blazingly angry. He would tolerate no hesitancy from General Ullrich, the commander of the *Viking Division*. *Viking* would advance through the minefield and the electrically charged wire whatever the casualties.

'Ullrich,' Gilles barked, 'you either attack or you name your successor!'

Ullrich was a proud man, who had fought a very hard, bitter war to become a divisional commander. He was not going to lose that command now. Heavy-hearted he summoned *Obersturmbannführer* Dorr, commander of the *SS Germania Regiment*, to his CP and ordered him to attack.

The big SS Colonel accepted the order without the slightest hesitation. That same evening he led his young volunteers into the minefields. They suffered terrible casualties, but Dorr allowed no retreat. He forced them forwards. They hit the electric wire barriers. The night was hideous with their screams as 20,000 volts racked the grenadiers' wildly thrashing bodies. Suddenly the darkness was split by the dramatic blue light of short circuits and heavy with the stink of burned flesh. And then they were through and the Russians were running for their lives. Behind them charred bundles of rags and flesh hung everywhere on the wrecked wires.

That morning, covered by Rudel's Me 262s flying at tree-top level, the Viking crossed the canal at Kaloz. Gilles at Corps HQ ordered a change of objective for the *4th SS*. Dunapentele would be left to the slower moving *3rd Panzer* on the right wing. The two SS armoured divisions would now make a bold dash for Budapest further up the river, with the Danube itself forming their right flank. *Viking* was commanded to drive for Ercsi, a matter of some twenty kilometres or so from the Hungarian capital. Now Gilles planned to seize Budapest in one bold stroke.

But by now Tolbuchin was reacting to the surprise attack. He threw in all his reserves, the best of the Guards divisions. The two forces met at the village of Sarosd. The point of the *Viking* was cut off within the shattered hamlet. The Division counter-attacked and freed the leading unit.

Hastily the regimental staff of the *Germania Regiment* which was leading the drive again, assembled to discuss the next move. But all Russian resistance in Sarosd was not yet crushed. Just as the officers were bending their shaven heads over the big maps, a lone Russian anti-tank gun, cunningly concealed in a shattered barn, opened up at pointblank range, blowing the Regiment's key officers apart in a fury of fire. *Obersturmbannführer* Dorr fell with the rest, wounded for the sixteenth time in combat. This time it was to be his final wound. Now Germania was without its commander and all its senior officers.

Still Gilles was determined to push on. The first refugees from Budapest, German and Hungarian, were beginning to trickle into the SS positions, bringing with them horrific tales of the tortures and cruelties being inflicted on the defenders and the civilians in their charge when they fell into Russian hands. They told Gilles too that the defenders were on their last legs; ammunition and food for the 800,000 civilians was beginning to run out very rapidly.

On the Monday of the new week, after the disastrous events in Sarosd, the *4th SS Corps* attacked again. Everywhere the word was passed from mouth to mouth. 'Today we reach Budapest!' It acted like magic on the eager young volunteers. They went into battle singing. A row of small villages were taken in a rush and the point of the *Viking* reached Adony on the Danube.

Marshal Tolbuchin began to panic. He had thrown all his reserves in by now, but still he had not stopped the Fritzes. In fact they had broken his 3rd Ukrainian Front in two at Adony. He called Lt-General Scharochin, commander of the 57th Rifle Army, which now stood in the Germans' path and warned him of the danger of his Army being encircled on the following day; would it not be better that he withdrew his Army across the Danube to the eastern bank?

Scharochin knew Tolbuchin of old. He recognized the suggestion of his Army Commander as a cunning device to exculpate himself. When the time came to analyse the causes of the disaster on that front, Tolbuchin would point the finger at him as the commander who had first ordered a major withdrawal. More scared of 'Old Leather Face', Stalin, in the far-off Kremlin than the enemy at his doorstep, Scharochin refused. He preferred to stand and fight on the next day. On 23 January, the point of the *Viking* attacked directly north on both sides of the River Danube. At first they made excellent progress, throwing back the 57th Rifle Army in confusion. Then a new enemy entered – the weather.

It started to snow, as if it would never cease again. In a matter of minutes, the roads and tracks that the tanks were using disappeared completely under the flying white deluge. Gunners and commanders were blinded. The massive 72-ton *Royal Tigers*, isolated in the whirling mass of snow, were easy meat for the Russian infantry, armed with their portable anti-tank weapons. The Germans began to suffer severe casualties, and their progress was charted in metres, not in the kilometres of the previous days.

Somewhere or other Scharochin found a whole tank corps. The tankers were young and armed with the old-fashioned T-34s instead of the new *Joseph Stalins*. But they were courageous.

To Scharochin's relief, the snow turned to fog. It gave his inexperienced tankers more of a chance against the Fritzes. Dug in at the hulldown position, exposing only their thick glacis plates, the T-34s, massed in troops of six and seven, waited for the Germans to loom out of the mist. The *Tigers* slaughtered the T-34s. But there was always one surviving Russian tank which could place that shell between turret and hull, or in the tracks, or in the engine cowling to bring the Fritz colossus to a final halt.

On 29 January, Scharochin, now actively encouraged by Tolbuchin, launched what was left of the young tank corps, supported by massive air cover, into a major attack against the *4th SS Corps* at the village of Petend.

The SS fought back desperately, but there was no holding the Russians now. They had scented blood. Scharochin forgot Stalin. He thought only of victory.

He threw in all his last reserves. Full of a double ration of vodka and the promise of loot, leave and women, once Budapest had fallen, they charged into battle, arms linked, their bands playing the old Czarist marches. The Germans mowed them down by their hundreds but still they came on. The SS faltered and started to crumble.

Desperately Gilles tried to shore up his front but to no avail. The SS divisions were bled white. The 'bodies', as he was wont to call them to his staff, were no longer there. The pace of the withdrawal quickened.

One hundred and eighty Soviet tanks appeared on the SS Corps' front to be opposed by exactly nine *Tigers* left to the *Death's Head* and fourteen still running in the *Viking*. There was nothing the SS men could do, but retreat. The Russians were everywhere.

On 1 February, 1945, Gilles, Commander of the *Fourth SS Panzer Corps*, reported to his chief, General Balck, that his divisions were exhausted. They could do no more.

Balck, who hated the Armed SS, but who at the same time knew that if the Third Reich's élite had failed to break through to the Hungarian capital there was no hope left, made his decision. It was very simple. Tolbuchin had won; he had lost. 'Gilles,' he ordered, 'prepare to withdraw!'

That same evening, what was left of the *Viking* and *Death's Head* began to move back from the Danube.

The last attempt to relieve Budapest had failed.

TWO

'Gentlemen;' SS *Obergruppenführer und General der Polizei und der Waffen SS* Pfeffer-Wildenbruch said with surprising formality in view of the fact that all the windows in his Buda HQ were long shattered and there was new snow drifting in through the shell-hole in the ceiling, 'please, be seated.'

The assembled commanders, General Rumohr of the *8th SS Cavalry*, General Zehender of the *22nd SS Cavalry*, Colonel Habicht, and their staffs sat down at the long, blanket-covered table.

Pfeffer-Wildenbruch began. 'The reason I have called you here today is to decide what we shall do next here in Buda. As you have all realized by now – even you must have Habicht – there will be no more attempts by our comrades to break through. We must assume that we have been written off by the High Command. In a way, that knowledge, gentlemen, is not as frightening as it sounds. For a change, we at the front can make our own decisions without reference to the Greatest Captain of all Times.'

The others laughed at the reference to Hitler, a bitter indication enough of just how much these powerful officers felt cut off from the Homeland.

'So we have the freedom of choice. The question is – how shall we exercise it? As I see it, gentlemen, there are perhaps three courses of action open to us. Let me first suggest the worst one – we could surrender to the Soviets.'

There was a groan of dismay from most of the high-ranking officers and Habicht, his face flushed, cried hotly, '*Never!*'

Pfeffer-Wildenbruch held up his hands for peace and said, 'I was merely playing the devil's advocate, gentlemen. The second alternative is that we rally what forces we have left to us and using your armour, Habicht, attempt to fight our way out.'

'May I say a word on that, Corps Commander?' General Zehender asked. 'In the cavalry divisions we probably have enough transport left and enough fuel to get most of the troopers out of Buda. However, what are we going to do about the auxiliaries? There are over two thousand of these females left in the city. Now I know what all you gentlemen think of these "field mattresses". Probably some of my younger officers have had personal experience of their undoubted charms and toughness' – he coughed suddenly – 'in the horizontal position.'

There was a rumble of soft laughter from the others.

'But when all that is said and done, they are German women and we cannot leave them behind to fall into Bolshevik hands. There again, I am not prepared to sacrifice valuable fighting manpower to find places in the vehicles for these non-productive females.'

'That leaves us with the third alternative,' Pfeffer-Wildenbruch intervened. 'We stay and fight it out with the Russians here in Buda. The question is – how?'

Habicht sprang to his feet, his face flushed with both anger and excitement. 'I shall tell you how, gentlemen,' he cried.

Pfeffer-Wildenbruch observed the officer with mild amusement. Even at this late hour the man was still seeking some desperate glory, while all that awaited them was death. 'Please be so kind as to do so, Habicht,' he remarked.

'Gentlemen, I think all of us know that we are not going to leave Buda alive,' Habicht began starkly. The faint smiles disappeared from his listeners' faces. 'Once we are aware of that, I suggest the rest is easy.'

Pfeffer-Wildenbruch sipped his drink and listened, but he felt a sudden quickening of his pulse at the prospect he knew the young crippled Colonel would hold out to them.

'There are two ways one can fight a siege, gentlemen,' Habicht continued. 'One can lie supinely like some fat whore with her legs open passively waiting to be taken. Or one can fight back against the rapist with tooth, nail, and claw.' His voice rose a little. 'We can make the Reds pay – and pay dearly – for every metre of territory they take. The defender in a built-up area is always at the advantage. For every casualty we take, we inflict four on the Reds. Buda can become a running sore on the side of the Red Army. As long as we are able to hold out here in Buda, Tolbuchin will not dare to penetrate deeper into Western Hungary.

'Gentlemen, we must not see ourselves as already dead and forgotten, but as men who are admittedly condemned to death but who are fighting against that sentence and making their fight visible to the world.' His voice was shaky with excitement now. 'Buda can well go down in German history, gentlemen, as another Kollwitz!'[1] Habicht knew by the looks on the faces of his listeners now, from general to staff lieutenant, that he had them.

'We must change our tactics. Instead of waiting passively for the Reds to attack, we must go over to the offensive. Small well-armed fighting patrols, led by the most aggressive officers and NCOs and guided by Hungarian volunteers, who know Buda like the backs of their hands, ferreting out Red CPs and HQs and destroying them. Larger groups working their way through the sewers and coming up in the Red lines of communications and creating panic and havoc there A surprise armour thrust towards Gellert Hill to destroy that damned artillery concentration up there.' He gasped for breath. 'That should be our aim, gentlemen,' he concluded, his face flushed crimson, to drive the Reds mad.

---

1. A famous siege in Prussian military history.

They will crush us in the end undoubtedly, but they will have to pay the price of their sanity to do so!'

Habicht's impassioned speech was received with excited chatter and comment. Pfeffer-Wildenbruch let the conference have its head for a few minutes; he let them talk, knowing how gullible the younger Armed SS officer was for such heady, exciting words. Of course, the man was a fanatic. Yet what alternative was left open to them?

Then he made up his mind. Tapping his glass on the table to attract their attention and that of the orderlies with the bottles, he waited until their glasses were filled once again. A little unsteadily he rose to his feet and gave them a sad, little, drunken smile, before raising his glass, knowing that very few of them would survive the next few days. 'Gentlemen, I give you a toast. To the last days of Buda!'

'To the last days of Buda!' they chorused as one and drank the fiery spirit in a swift gulp. Next instant glass after glass was shattered against the wall as if to symbolize the final destruction soon to come.

THREE

The company-sized NKVD patrol caught them at dawn, just as they were emerging from the sewer. Schulze's group had carried out a very successful raid that night, destroying a whole vehicle park of the 7th Mechanical Corps, without a single casualty. But obviously one of the many communist infiltrators, who were now everywhere among the Hungarian civilian population in German-held Buda, had betrayed them. The NKVD murder specialists, who were dug in among the shattered ruins all around the square where *Europa* patrols generally left the great underground sewage system, waited until the full patrol of some thirty men emerged; then they opened up with their automatic weapons.

It was a massacre. On all sides the young Europeans fell on to the suddenly blood-red snow, screaming for help in their own languages and the one word of German they all knew – HILFE!'

But there was no help to be won. The god of Colonel Habicht's 'holy crusade against the heathen Bolshevik' was deaf to entreaty. The NKVD systematically slaughtered the young SS men, trapped in the ruined square. Then the fire stopped as suddenly as it had started, and Schulze, hidden behind a body next to Chink realized why. There was a sudden whoosh like a dragon's breath and a monstrous sheet of evil blue flame hissed across the heaving pile of young bodies. '*Flame thrower!*' Chink screamed in a paroxysm of fear.

'Come on,' Schulze cried. 'The sewer!'

The flamethrower spoke again. Behind them as they ran crazily for the entrance, the human bodies began to blaze. Slugs beat a pattern around their flying feet. Without the slightest hesitation, Schulze dived head-first down the stinking hole, his fall softened by the noxious, unthinkable brown deposit which lined the bottom of the dark shaft. Next instant, Chink fell beside him.

They dodged away from the entrance just in time. The first dark shapes of grenades came hurtling down. They exploded with a tremendous, ear-splitting noise, magnified tenfold by the round echoing shaft. Red-hot, razor-sharp fragments of steel flew through the narrow confines of the tunnel, whining off the dripping, lime-encrusted walls. The two survivors of the ill-fated patrol blundered blindly away from the entrance and the cloud of poison gas that was already being pumped down the shaft.

The ill-fated patrol was the third that Schulze had led that week, each worse than the previous one. Habicht gave the Regiment no rest. Every hour of every day brought fresh deaths and fresh casualties. The regimental hospital, the cellars of a shattered store, was a crowded scene of butchery. Above ground the streets were littered with *Europa*'s dead and the charred, burnt-out wrecks of their vehicles, the result of Habicht's dynamic, unrelenting aggressiveness.

Now, as Schulze and Chink, their chests heaving wildly, sat in the stinking shaft, well away from the scene of the ambush, listening to the scampering of the huge, pink-eyed rats which were everywhere, the big Sergeant-Major realized that, at last, he had had enough. He handed the Chink the damp remainder of his last cigarette and sighed, 'The time has come for Mrs Schulze's boy to get back to Hamburg and Mother.'

'Chink, he come with, yes?'

'Yes, Chink he come with,' Schulze answered wearily, 'but Christ knows how.'

'Howabout shit-Jewboy?' Chink suggested. 'He got us in – he get us out.'

Schulze sat in thought for a moment. He knew that the Regiment's days were numbered and that Germany was nearly finished. The Russians were already in East Prussia and the Tommies and Amis in the Eifel fighting their way to the Rhine. The time had come to save his skin. He made up his mind. Wearily he got to his feet. 'Come on Chink, let's get out of this shitheap and back to the Regiment.'

'And then?'

'Then,' Schulze grinned at him suddenly, 'we go and find the Jewboy.'

Two hours later Schulze reported to Habicht in his cellar CP. 'They did not die in vain,' he said fervently when Schulze was finished. 'They died for the cause of Europe. Rest assured, Schulze, that one day they will be remembered.'

'Ballocks', Schulze thought. He'd had a bellyful of the Hawk's fanaticism. All he wanted to hear now was, 'The war's over. It's peace!'

'Well, Schulze, I expect you're beat. See if the cooks still have anything for you to eat, then get some sleep.'

'Before I go, sir,' Schulze said slowly, 'I'd like to report something.'

'What?'

'Just before we were jumped in that square, I thought I heard the sound of tanks off in the direction of Kobanyai Street.'

'Tanks?' Habicht said eagerly. 'They must have been Red. Ours are all wrecked.' He strode across the cellar to the big street map of Buda and peered at it for a moment. 'Kobanyai Street is well within the Red-held sector. I think the 8th Cavalry must have lost it last week.'

Wearily Schulze clicked his heels together and played his new role. 'Request permission to select my own patrol and go out tonight and destroy those tanks?'

The Hawk swung round, his single eye gleaming excitedly. 'Permission granted, Schulze. Pick whoever you like.'

Schulze pushed aside with a grim smile the blanket and went out.

Down the ruined streets of Occupied Buda, the refugees poured eastwards, backs bent under their pathetic bundles of possessions. Bearded Jews, who had somehow managed to survive the German persecution, in worn black frock coats; Hungarian aristocrats in their shredded finery; workers in overalls and quilted jackets; furtive deserters from the Hungarian Army, their uniforms hidden beneath tattered old coats. Everyone was attempting to leave the capital before the final attack on the German positions.

The refugees provided excellent cover for Schulze and Chink and the hand-picked patrol of trusted SS men as they emerged from the sewer system into the winter dusk. Schulze led his men through the maze of streets following the map he had imprinted on his memory, directing them skilfully through the flood of civilians.

Finally they reached their destination: Kobanyai Street. It was different from the other roads they had passed along. It was empty of refugees and the cellars beneath the rubble were still occupied. Schulze could tell that from the smoke emerging from their on chimneys which poked up everywhere from the ruins.

'All right men, spread out. You two Cheeseheads, get yourselves under cover at the head of the street. And keep down if you spot any Ivans. I don't want any trouble tonight. You Frogs get up to the other end and dig yourselves in on both sides of the road.' The Frenchmen sped away.

Schulze detailed the two remaining Danes to act as bodyguard and the little group began to check out the cellars.

At first they were unsuccessful. The cellars were crammed with gypsies and peasants from the surrounding countryside who had moved in once the owners had fled before the Russian attack. They had never heard of Csoki.

But just as Schulze was beginning to believe that the old Jewish pedlar had already made his escape from the doomed city, he found an old woman who knew him.

'The little chocolate drop?' she echoed the name, staring up at the soldiers quite unafraid. 'Yes, I saw him yesterday.'

'Where is he?' Schulze asked eagerly.

'Two cellars further,' she answered readily and then for some totally unfathomable reason she began to laugh. She was still laughing when Chink knocked on the shrapnel-splintered door of the cellar indicated.

A boy opened the door. Over Chink's shoulder, Schulze caught a quick glimpse of an untidy kitchen, with children playing on the dirty floor, a woman with dark nervous eyes checking a girl's hair for lice, with beyond a dark hunched figure in priest's robes, sitting at a wooden table, eating a pork sandwich and reading his holy book.

Then a woman appeared. Didn't they know the Russians would shoot her, if they learned she had spoken to a German patrol. She threw up her hands in nervous extravagance. 'God preserve us from the Germans and the Jews,' she exclaimed.

'Amen!' the figure at the table said solemnly, without taking his eyes off the book.

'We'll cause no trouble, Mother,' Schulze said appeasingly. 'All we're looking for is a man called Csoki. We were told he might be here.'

'Never heard of him,' the woman said decisively and made to slam the door in their faces.

'Wait,' the figure at the table commanded. 'Did you say Csoki?'

'I did,' Schulze said eagerly.

The priest said something quickly in Magyar. Reluctantly the woman stood aside and let them pass into the kitchen. She closed the door hastily after them and said in German: 'They'll bring us trouble, take my word for it, Monsignor.'

'The door of God's house is always open, my child,' he said gently. Slowly he turned to face them and Schulze's mouth dropped open as he recognized the man in the long black robe.

Behind him Chink gasped. 'It's the Yid!'

FOUR

Janosz the Pedlar had changed since they had last seen him. His beard had gone and he no longer appeared as old. His face had fattened out and he had definitely got a small paunch, which went well with his new role of a good-living Churchman. Indeed all in all, it looked very much as if Janosz had not done too badly for himself since he had arrived in the capital.

Schulze swallowed the last of his sandwich, washed it down with a mighty slug of the wine and turned to the 'priest'.

'Come off it, you old hypocrite. What are you doing here, togged up like the sodding Pope, eh?'

'What can a poor Jew do?' he said softly and shrugged eloquently. 'It's the best cover imaginable, Schulze. Those Russian soldier boys might be communist, but they're peasant first and they've got a lot of respect for a man of the cloth. It is surprising where one can go in Budapest when one is a Monsignor! But what do you want from me, Schulze?'

'You know what you said back there after we had crossed the river? Well, I and a few of the boys want out. We're finished here. We want to be gone before the end comes.'

Janosz seemed pleased. 'You have come just at the right time, Schulze. In twenty-four hours I am going to make my own departure too. I have what I came here to Buda to find, my fare to Palestine.' He opened the breviary and took out a small envelope. Very carefully he let its contents fall on the opened pages. Perhaps two or three dozen stamps tumbled out.

'Your fare?' Schulze queried puzzled.

'Yes.' Janosz smiled. 'Doesn't seem much to you, does it, eh?' He picked up one of them carefully by the edge. 'A five pound orange on blue paper, worth perhaps four hundred British pounds.'

'You get money for stamps?' Chink said incredulously.

'Very much so, my Chinese friend. Hide them in the lapel of your jacket, say, or in its lining and you carry a fortune with you, able to turn it into any currency you like and in any country.'

Chink's dark eyes gleamed with undisguised admiration.

'Can you take me and a few of my fellows with you?' Schulze persisted.

'How many?'

Schulze told him and he thought for a moment. 'Yes, that would about do it, my friend.'

'Do what?'

Janosz hesitated for a fraction of a second. 'Schulze, my fare was paid by a certain number of citizens of this city who want to escape.'

'Why pay you?'

'What do you mean, Schulze?'

'I mean they are fleeing by the thousand out there. Why should they pay you anything to do the same?'

Janosz beamed at him, as if he were a stupid child, who at long last was asking a reasonably intelligent question. 'All those people you have seen are going east. My people want to go *west*. They are the kind of people who will not survive long in the glorious new socialist republic that will soon be founded here in Hungary.'

Schulze nodded his understanding. 'Now I get you. But how are you going to do it?'

'By courtesy of Comrade Marshal Tolbuchin of the Second Ukrainian Front.'

Schulze sat up in amazement.

'I saw him two days ago and he gave me permission to move my – er – flock out of danger. It was a true expression of Christian charity.' Janosz made a gesture as if counting money. 'A train of three coaches and room for 180 people at 1,000 silver forints a person.' He shrugged. 'Even Soviet marshals are not immune apparently to the temptations of capital, eh?'

'So it would seem,' Schulze said drily.

'We are all bound – God willing – for Palestine; you see, all the passengers will be Jews.'

'But how the hell are you going to get to Palestine via the east?' Schulze protested.

'We are not going east. We are going west. Of course, the good Marshal does not know that. You see Schulze, I do not trust our Soviet friend. I feel that once we have handed over the money to him and we are safely out of the immediate area of Budapest, travelling eastwards; we are going to suffer an unfortunate accident.'

'What do you mean?' Schulze asked.

'The train will be attacked by partisans, rogue Cossacks, who knows what? But attacked we will be and the good Marshal will ensure that we go no further as living evidence of the little grease he has taken, and then he will loot our bodies for further gain.'

'My God !' Schulze exploded in sheer admiration. 'You think of everything!'

'I am a Jew,' Janosz said, as if that were sufficient explanation.

'That is why it is opportune that you have appeared now, Schulze.'

'Why?'

'Because I would like to hire you and your good friends of the Armed SS to protect the train on its journey westwards against the dangers that face us.'

'*Hire a unit of the Armed SS to protect a trainload of Yids!*' Schulze looked incredulous.

'It is my last chance to get to Palestine, Schulze, I must take every precaution. Now listen. Admiral Horthy's[1] armoured train is still in the sidings at Buda main station. The locomotive and

---

1. The recently deposed dictator of Hungary.

the carriages are all armoured and have machine-gun-turrets and that sort of thing. You'll probably know what I mean? Now for a large consideration – and as we have already obtained a clearance from the good Marshal to leave Buda – the station master of Buda Station will let us have that train, already fuelled and with a trusted driver at the controls. Again for a large consideration, the rail track staff at Buda and throughout Western Hungary will ensure that the train passes safely into Austria.'

'You mean they're going to arrange it so that the train doesn't go east, as the Ivans expect, but westwards?'

'Exactly. My plan is to pass through Western Hungary into Austria, which is still in German hands. Hopefully, Christian charity will still prevail there among your fellow countrymen – at a price naturally – so that we will be able to continue into Italy. There with luck, the British and their new Italian allies will not stop us getting to the port. The Hagannah –'

'The what?'

'A Jewish underground organization to which I happen to belong.'

'*You* would,' Schulze said, completely mesmerized by the little Jew.

'As I was saying, the Hagannah will ensure that there is a ship organized for us to run the British blockade off Palestine.' He paused and looked up at the big NCO expectantly. 'What do you think, Sergeant-Major?'

'I think – what do we get out of it?'

'A free trip out of this hell-hole.'

'Not enough, Yid,' the Chink said before Schulze could speak. 'You pretty shit-smart man. You pay more.'

'Yes,' Schulze grunted 'What's in it for us?'

'One kilo of coffee, a half bottle of schnapps, one carton of cigarettes – American,' Janosz said, his eyes on the ground sadly like a man whose heart had just been broken. 'Per soldier.'

'Make it two cartons and you're on?'

'One American – and one Turkish?' Janosz asked swiftly.

'Done!'

'Good!' Janosz beamed at him and stuck out his skinny hand. 'You will receive them on the day.'

'And when is that?' Schulze asked.

'Tomorrow night, at eight.'

'Where?'

'We assemble in the yard of the old locomotive factory. You will meet us there with your men in Russian uniform. It is better.'

'We'll get it,' Schulze said and rose to go. As the woman extinguished the light so that they could pass out unnoticed into the darkness, Monsignor Janosz intoned in his most saintly voice, 'And may Jesus Christ, Our Lord, watch over you, my son.'

'Ballocks!' was 'his son's' sole reply.

FIVE

On the following morning, 12 February, 1945, Marshal Tolbuchin launched his final assault on the German SS divisions grouped around the *Burg* in Buda.[1] Heedless of the civilians still there, he began a massive two-hour long artillery bombardment as a preliminary to his advance.

One after another the German strongpoints at the University, the museum, the radio station were knocked out and the surviving SS men sent streaming back to dig in furiously elsewhere. The bombardment ended as abruptly as it had started and the T-34s – hundreds of them, supported by infantry – began to move in.

For a couple of hours, a group of SS men from the *8th Cavalry* managed to hold the Moricz Zsigmond Square against a huge force of Soviet tanks and Guards infantry. But in the end they broke too and fled towards the old castle, which dominated Castle Hill, and was the main German headquarters.

Made cautious by the defence of the square, which had cost him twenty tanks and a hundred Guards killed, the commander of the Narva Tank Regiment, leading the attack, radioed his HQ for artillery support.

To the surprise of the German interception experts crouched over their radios in the castle's ancient cellars, Marshal Tolbuchin

---

1. Also known as Castle Hill.

himself replied from somewhere on the other side of the Danube. 'The hour of decision has come,' he barked over the air. 'Now we must chop the paws off the German beast. Comrade Colonel – attack now, or don't bother to come back here!' The threat was undisguised and the commander of the Narva Regiment knew it. He threw in his tanks.

At their posts all around the Castle, the men of the *8th* and *22nd SS* and of the *Europa*, watched open-mouthed as the T-34s started to crawl up the twisting, turning streets which led to the heights. On all four sides the heights were black with the crawling metal monsters. It was as if a ring of steel were about to garrotte them to death. The SS commanders knew that their young soldiers might well panic and break, if nothing were done. General Rumohr, who like General Zehender and Colonel Habicht had taken up his place in the fortified line, grabbed a *panzerfaust* out of the hands of a mesmerized grenadier. 'Follow me!' he shouted, springing out into the open.

A handful of his staff followed. Tearing down the hill, he stopped a hundred metres away from the nearest T-34. Standing completely in the open, ignoring the tracer cutting the air wildly all around, he aimed as calmly as if he were standing at some peacetime range. Blue flame jetted from the back of the anti-tank weapon. The long wooden projectile with its squat round metal head wobbled clumsily through the air. In the same moment that a burst of Soviet fire cut Rumohr down, the bomb exploded directly underneath the tank's turret. At that short range, the impact was tremendous. An instant later the bomb exploded and the turret rose into the air. Within seconds the rump was a sea of greedy red flames.

Rurnohr's sacrifice broke the spell. Everywhere the young grenadiers opened up with their *panzerfaust* weapons. The air was suddenly full of the awkward projectiles. Tank after tank was hit, its covering infantry running wildly for the safety of the nearest house, tracked by German machine-gun fire. But still they kept on. It seemed Regiment Narva had an inexhaustible supply of T-34s. Slowly the *panzerfausts* began to give out.

Deep in his cellar HQ, filled with dead and dying grenadiers a drunk, desperate Pfeffer-Wildenbruch asked for volunteers to tackle the tanks with adhesive bombs. But there were no men left to volunteer, save the wounded and the medical personnel. In the end it was the men of the X-ray unit, pale-faced bespectacled medics, who seized the sticky bombs and went out to do battle with the metal monsters.

The 'X-Ray Commandos', as they called themselves during their short-lived existence, proved themselves bold, daring infantrymen. Perhaps it was because they did not realize the risks they were running. Time and time again one of them would dart out of the rubble and stick his bomb to the side of a T-34. The hollow clang of metal adhering to metal would alarm the Russian crew and they would swing their machine-guns round to deal with their attacker in one swift burst of fire. But there was nothing they could do about the bomb stuck to their metal side like a deadly limpet. A few managed to bail out, but only a very few. The rest remained in their battened down vehicle and waited for death with almost stoical resignation.

Within the hour the slope was littered with the bloody white-robed figures of the 'X-Ray Commando' among the smoking burning hulks. But the Russians still kept coming on. General Zehender's remaining positions were overrun. His *SS Cavalry* had no heavy weapons left to stop the tanks. The tankers ground their 30-ton vehicles round and round over the SS men's slit trenches until the sides began to give in and the whole weight of their T-34s descended upon the terrified screaming men below. When they emerged their tracks were red with blood. Zehender's *SS Cavalry* started to break. Here and there, panic-stricken young soldiers dropped their weapons, sprang out of their holes and raised their hands in surrender to the advancing Russian infantry.

Angrily Zehender attempted to stop the rot. 'Get down you bastards!' he cried and sent a furious burst from his machine-pistol flying over the heads of the men with the raised hands.

The Russian infantry concentrated their fire on the man who had suddenly appeared only a hundred metres away, dressed in the uniform of an SS general. He didn't seem to notice. He kept firing at his own men running towards the advancing Russians, his heavy face flushed an angry red. The first slug struck him. He staggered, but kept after his men, crying, 'Come, back, come back, do you hear?'

Another bullet hit him. He staggered badly. The machine-pistol fell from his hands and he sank to his knees. 'Come back,' he cried desperately, the tears rolling down his cheeks.

'*General!*' a Russian in an earth-coloured blouse cried and pointed his tommy-gun in the direction of the dying German.

'Capture him and he's good for a medal and fourteen days' leave.' The infantry surged forward with a guttural '*urrah!*'

Zehender seemed to understand. His fingers fumbled with his pistol holster. Somehow or other he managed to get the Walther out. With a hand that trembled visibly, he raised the wavering pistol, placed the muzzle against his right temple, pressed the trigger and his head disappeared in a sudden spurt of scarlet.

After this sacrifice the heart finally ebbed from the German defenders of the hill. It would not be long before what was left of them started to surrender.

Habicht put down his glasses. 'Schulze,' he cried above the roar of the Soviet artillery.

'Sir.' Schulze dropped to his knees next to the Colonel outside the dugout CP.

'The Cavalry are having a very bad time of it,' Habicht said. 'They're taking tremendous losses: We must help them.'

Schulze looked at him in alarm. The three or four hundred survivors of the *Europa* were in a good position. There they could be overrun and taken prisoner without too many casualties. Schulze thought he had done his duty by the men; now it was time that he and his little picked band should make their way to the loco-motive works. 'What do you mean – help them?'

Habicht did not seem to notice that he had omitted the 'sir'. 'A flank attack. That is what is required. We could catch them off their guard. We'd be through them like a hot knife through butter. The Red bastards think they've got it all worked out. But they haven't reckoned with the *Europa*, have they Schulze?'

'Did you say – flank attack?'

'Yes.' Already Habicht was surveying his front, working out a rudimentary swift plan of attack. 'We'll go in on both sides, taking him down there where –'

'But goddamit, they've got a score of tanks down there to our front!' Schulze exploded. 'How in Christ's name are we going to break through them? – *with tin openers?*'

Suddenly Habicht became aware that the Regimental Sergeant-Major was shouting at him, his face crimson with rage, the veins standing out at his temples an angry red. 'Why are you talking in this manner?' he demanded coldly.

Schulze gasped for air. 'Because you're crazy!'

Habicht glared at him, his hand falling to his pistol holster. 'You mean you intend to disobey my order, Sarnt-Major?' he yelled.

'Of course, I do, you stupid bastard!' Schulze yelled back, beside himself with rage, not caring any longer. 'Flank attack. What good will that do? We're finished – *kaput!*' He swallowed hard. 'Let them surrender, run away, disperse, do any goddamn thing they like.' He indicated the men dug in all around with a furious sweep of his big hand. 'But don't make them die – NOW!'

Habicht's fingers fumbled with the flap of the holster, but the big NCO did not allow him to complete the movement. His boot lashed out and the pistol went flying from Habicht's hand. He yelped with pain and cried, 'This is mutiny, Schulze!'

'Of course it is. You have had your day, Habicht. Let them go. If you want to die – then die.' He extended his hand towards the Russian positions.

'*Die?*' Habicht echoed the words, his face completely mad now. 'Of course – *die.*'

Words died on Schulze's lips as Habicht pushed by him and ran down the slope towards the Russians. The enemy reacted at once. Bullets whined all around the running man, but he seemed to bear a charmed life. Nothing seemed able to touch him. He kept running and screaming that one final word '*die…die…die…*' Suddenly he faltered. A burst of Russian tommy-gun had ripped his skinny chest open. He struggled on a few more paces. Another burst slammed cruelly into his stomach. Still he staggered on, his legs giving beneath him. 'DIE!' he screamed one last time in a voice that made the hairs on Schulze's neck rise in terror. And then he slumped face forward on to the pitted snow without another sound.

For one long moment an echoing silence seemed to descend upon the battlefield. Even the Russians seemed to hesitate, as if awed by the manner of the Hawk's death. Then Schulze pulled himself together, clapped his big hands around his mouth, and cried to the young volunteers crouching around him, 'Bugger off, lads! It's all over. Go home while you've still got a chance.'

The boys in their holes did not move.

'Bugger off, I say, get back to your mothers, you stupid young sods!' Schulze yelled, his eyes wild with rage.

Still they did not move. Schulze could not wait any longer. He had his own plans. He fired a furious burst at the *Europa* regimental flag still flying proudly over the CP. The pole splintered. Slowly the flag began to descend to the ground.

It did the trick. The survivors of *SS Regiment Europa* broke. Screaming and shouting in half a dozen languages, they fled, fighting and clawing at each other in sudden panic, running desperately from the men in earth-coloured blouses who were now beginning to advance on their abandoned positions. The great 'European' dream was dead.

Schulze doubled up the hill towards the ruined tram shed in which he had positioned the men he was taking with him. The floor of the shabby blue tram was lined with sandbags and the windows covered with corrugated iron sheeting, with slits cut in it for their weapons.

Schulze took it all in in a glance. 'All right, Cheesehead, get in.' The big Dutchman swung himself up into the cab and grabbed the twin brass steering handles in his big paws.

'Are you ready, the rest of you!' Schulze yelled above the hoarse triumphant cries of the advancing Russians.

'Ready!' the men, waiting to push the tram out of the wrecked shed cried back.

'*Now!*' Schulze bellowed and jumped in, Schmeisser at the ready.

The young men heaved. The train started to move. 'More!' Schulze bellowed.

The men shoved with all their strength. The tram edged out of the shed. Ahead of it stretched the steep twisting cobbled street, packed with advancing Russians. The men to the rear gave one last shove and scrambled hastily to swing themselves aboard. The old tram started to gather speed. The Russians were not slow to react. Bullets howled off the metal sideplates. At the driver's side, Schulze swung his Schmeisser from side to side, hosing the Russians with lead. A group of soldiers caught unawares went flying out of the way, save one. The tram lurched unpleasantly and for one awful moment Schulze thought it was going to stop. But it continued its crazy progress, leaving behind it a dead Russian on the tracks, his head and legs grotesquely amputated.

They swung round another bend and before them loomed a hill which Schulze knew they would never get up. But they were through the Russians by now and the nearest entrance to the sewer system was only fifty metres or so away. It was time to go. As the tram began to lose speed, Schulze slung his machine-pistol and yelled, 'All right, it's time to abandon ship. Come on Chink, let's go.' Two minutes later the whole bunch of them were entering the sewers.

SIX

Budapest was dying in flames, but the anxious group of middle-aged Jewish men and women had no eyes now for the city in which they had been born and spent half their lives. Budapest was the past. They saw only the future, symbolized by the ugly black armoured behemoth steaming in front of them on the siding.

'Well?' Janosz demanded, obviously proud of his achievement, 'what do you think, Sergeant-Major?'

Schulze took a long look at the locomotive, the three coaches and the little guards van at the back, which would be occupied by the SS. It looked good. The locomotive had three-centimetre thick armour and a heavy iron reinforced prow to cut through any obstruction. The coaches were similarly armoured, with slits and gun-ports running their length, while the guards van, armoured too, had a raised towerlike structure on its roof, in which a machine-gunner and a look-out could be posted to cover the length of the coaches' roofs. 'Excellent,' he said. 'But with all that armour, it's going to be slow, isn't it?'

'Yes,' a guttural Magyar voice answered the question for him, 'at the most thirty kilometres an hour.'

Schulze swung round. A squat man in greasy overalls stood there, wiping his oily hands in a piece of cotton waste.

'Attila Pal, the driver,' the Jew said.

'Christ, what next?' Schulze exclaimed. 'Now we've got Attila the Hun on board too.'

We'll hit plenty of snow and more than likely get stuck,' the driver grumbled. 'Then the switches will be frozen up and we'll have to thaw them out before we can go on. And I don't know if I've enough sand in the sandbox to scatter under the driving wheels on a slippery slope. And God on high only knows what would happen if the fire in the firebox went out, the pipes would freeze and burst.' He shook his dark head sadly. 'It's not going to be easy at all.'

Schulze looked at him in awe, impressed by such unremitting pessimism. 'Christ! what do you do for laughs – go and visit the cemetery? Get into that cab of yours and raise steam; we'd better get out of here before some nosey Popov comes checking up.'

Janosz hurried the last of his 'flock' into the coaches and followed up the steps himself. In front the locomotive, shuddered as it let off steam. 'Well, my friend, we're ready to go. Palestine ahead.' He smiled at Schulze. 'We've done it.'

Schulze shook his head. 'Palestine ahead, what would the Führer say?'

Five minutes later the train left the dying city behind. Budapest was finished.

On the hill the battle entered its final stages. As the Russians swarmed into the old castle, General Pfeffer-Wildenbruch ordered the sweating radio-operator to send the *9th SS Mountain Corps'* last message.

It read: 'After fifty-two days of heroic battle, the Armed SS must end the fight this day. Peoples of Europe whom we once defended against the attacks of the Asiatic barbarians listen to the alarm bells now ringing in Budapest. It will be your turn next.'

There was a burst of automatic fire from the next room and someone screamed out in agony. The radio operator's finger hesitated on the key wet with his own blood.

'Carry on,' the drunken Corps Commander ordered, drawing his pistol.

The radio operator completed the message: 'Remember us Europe, for we have died for you.'

The next moment the door caved in and a horde of firing soldiers poured through. Far away in Berlin, the operator who had picked up the message heard a long continuous buzz.

Then there was only silence.

THE ARMOURED TRAIN

ONE

During the night the train had left the plain surrounding Budapest unnoticed by the Russians, and was climbing slowly into the mountains, chugging gently through a long, fir-wooded valley. Snow was falling, not too many kilometres ahead.

In the firecab, Attila the Hun, assisted by a fireman called 'Gypsy', divided his attention between the controls and the weather. He did not want to be caught on an ascent in new snow. 'More coal,' he barked to the fireman. 'Move your lazy Gypsy ass!'

'Cracking the whip again?' Schulze said cheerfully, dropping down on the swaying cinder-littered metal floor of the cab from the tender. 'How we doing?'

'Lousy.'

'What's wrong now?'

'That's wrong.' Attila pointed to the grey sky ahead. 'If that lot comes down on us while we're on a gradient like this, with the weight we've got to pull, then we could be in trouble. There are still a hundred kilometres to go before we're out of Russian-held territory.'

Schulze swung himself back on to the tender and began to pick his way over the heaped-up coal towards the first coach. The refugees had just finished eating their breakfasts when Schulze flung open the door for an instant and let in the freezing air. They raised their heads with the look of alarm common to the persecuted.

'Anything wrong, Schulze?' Janosz asked.

'Not much, but that happy-go-lucky Magyar at the wheel seems to think its going to snow again soon – and that's bad according to him.'

Janosz nodded his understanding. 'Please sit down, Schulze, I'd like to show you something.' Schulze sat down at the table opposite him and Janosz pulled out a map from his robe and spread it on the tables Western Hungary is occupied up to here, beyond Stuhlweissenburg, by the Russians, though your people are back in charge in the town itself I am informed. Now, if we continue as present we shall run to the north of Stuhlweissenburg, along the northern bank of Lake Balaton to where the main Russian frontline is located – here at Hidekut. Or so my informant at Russian HQ tells me.'

'Another recipient of Christian charity?' Schulze said mockingly, rubbing his thumb and forefinger together.

'Problem number one is to get there quickly before Marshal Tolbuchin finds out that we have gone westwards and not eastwards. Problem number two will be how to get through the front. But we'll worry about that one when –'

His words were drowned by a screeching, banging clamour as the train started to slow down, the bumpers banging into each other.

'Shit, what's up now?' Schulze cried and grabbing his machine pistol, he doubled out and dropped on to the snow at the side of the train, as the coaches came to a stop. 'All out there,' he yelled at the men peering out of the door of the guards van. 'Gunners man the turrets.' The big NCO ran through the deep snow to the locomotive. What's wrong, sunshine?' he cried up at the driver, who was fumbling with the controls.

'The steam regulator,' Attila called down. 'Perhaps the retainer nut has come off.'

Anxiously Schulze looked up at him. 'Is it serious?'

'Five or ten minutes. But we'd better get it started before the snow starts. On this slope and with this weight, it could be damned difficult to get it started otherwise.'

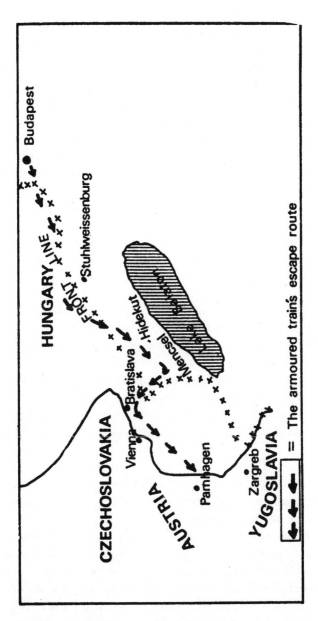

Budapest

HUNGARY LINE

FRONT

•Stuhlweissenburg

Lake Balaton

Hidekut

Mencsel

Bratislava

CZECHOSLOVAKIA

Vienna

AUSTRIA

Parnhagen

Zargreb

YUGOSLAVIA

= The armoured train's escape route

MAP 2: The escape route from Budapest – February, 1945

153

Schulze ran back to the van, where the men not manning the turret were assembled, shivering a little in the icy air after the pleasant hothouse fug of the van. 'You Frogs!' he rapped, 'get yourselves up to the front of the train and keep guard over that Magyar maniac at the controls. At the double now! Pat and Patichon,' Schulze said to the two Danes, 'you follow me.'

Together the three of them, weapons at the ready, swung round to the other side, conscious of the scared eyes watching them everywhere from the coaches as they headed for the thick fir forest which fringed the track. Down below there was a heavy silence, broken only by the steady whack of Attila's hammer. The men split up, on the look-out for partisans.

In spite of his confident grin, Schulze was worried. Attila had been right. Any moment now, it would start snowing and that would spell disaster.

Pat the Dane was caught off his guard. He had just rested his Schmeisser between his knees when a sudden slither of snow dislodged from one of the firs alerted him to the danger. Less than three metres away, a bearded, wolfish face under a shaggy black fur cap was smiling at him cruelly. The partisan had a knife, raised ready to throw, in his hand. There was no time to level his Schmeisser. The Dane acted instinctively. His right hand grabbed a handful of the frozen snow and in that same instant, flung it at the partisan's wolfish evil face. It caught him off balance. The knife aimed for the unsuspecting sentry's heart struck him in the shoulder. He yelped with sudden agony, but the searing pain did not stop him diving forward. His good shoulder thumped hard into the attacker's stomach.

The partisan went down with a gasp. He reacted instinctively: his hands reached up and grabbed the knife stuck in Pat's shoulder. The Dane screamed as the man snatched it out ready to strike again. But he knew he must overcome the pain. He was fighting for his life. His hands sought and found the partisan's shabby fur jacket. In that same moment he flung himself backwards with all his remaining strength and with his back supported by the snow, he rammed both his heavy boots straight into the other man's stomach. He screamed and went flying over the prostrate Dane's head.

Pat was on his feet first. His head swimming wildly, his vision blurred, he grabbed his Schmeisser, just as the groaning partisan attempted to get up. He pressed the trigger. At that short range, the wild burst virtually sawed the partisan in half. He collapsed against a tree trunk, trailing bright-red blood after him.

The burst of fire acted as a signal. Suddenly the wood was full of hoarse cries in Russian and Magyar, as the partisans started to run from cover. Pat, his eyes glazed, swung his Schmeisser from side to side, backing out of the trees into the open.

A bullet struck him just after he had cleared them. He dropped to one knee, his pale young face contorted with agony. Still he kept on firing. Then the Schmeisser tumbled from his limp fingers and he pitched forwards into the snow and lay very still.

Schulze reacted at once. 'Patichon back off – move towards the train. At the double!'

From the shelter of the trees, the partisans poured a stream of inaccurate fire at the two figures sprinting across the gleaming white surface of the snow. Suddenly the armoured train opened up as the twin Spandaus were brought to bear on the wood. At a rate of 700 rounds a minute, the slugs tore into the trees in one long, high-pitched burr. The partisans went down everywhere, falling in agony among the flying wood chips and the severed branches. Schulze made the cab. He reached up and sounded the steam whistle. The signal for all his men to withdraw.

'Get moving!' he yelled to Attila.

The Hungarian eased open the throttle, just as the first howling grey wave of snowflakes enveloped the train, covering the rails in an instant. There was the hiss of escaping steam and the metallic chatter of racing wheels. But nothing happened. The driving wheels were not gripping.

Attila rapped out an angry order to the fireman. Outside the snow was so thick now that Schulze could no longer see the advancing partisans and he knew his turret machine-gunners would be firing blind. The fireman jerked at a wire above his head. Schulze knew he was opening the sandbox, which allowed sand to drop on the track around the driving wheels. He said a quick prayer that this time the wheels would grip, just as the first dark shape of a partisan loomed up out of the whirling grey gloom.

He ripped off a burst. The partisan was bowled over screaming, as if he had been punched by a gigantic invisible fist. Behind Schulze, Attila eased the throttle open once more, hoping against hope that the sand had not already been dissipated in the new snow.

'Look out!' the fireman cried wildly.

Schulze swung round. A dark shape was clambering across the heaped coal of the tender, the whirling, grey-filled wind tugging at his clothes. In that confined space Schulze could not fire for fear of ricochets. He let the Schmeisser drop to his chest by its strap, and seized a piece of thick pine firewood. It whirled madly through the air and caught the partisan in the chest, just as he was about to jump down. He disappeared screaming over the side.

Behind Schulze Attila opened the throttle more. Slugs were pattering along the whole length of the train now. This was their last chance. The driving wheels spun on the slick rails. The laboured puffing of the engine increased. Clouds of smoke belched from the stack. In the howling gloom outside a grenade exploded in a burst of angry scarlet. Shrapnel howled off the metal side of the cab. A face appeared at Schulze's feet. His heavy 'dice-beaker' crashed into it. The partisan disappeared into the snowstorm. '*Come on! Come on!*' Schulze cried, leaning his body forward, urging the locomotive forward physically.

Slowly the wheels bit. Attila gave the locomotive more power. She started to move forward. The green needle on the speedometer began to creep upwards. As the armoured train's speed increased, the hail, of fire against her steel sides diminished. Sergeant-Major Schulze leaned weakly against the cab side and gasped, 'Never do that again, Attila. I've just pissed myself.'

TWO

The whole staff was drunk, with the exception of the Marshal himself and the Commander of the Grey Eagles, who was still brooding over his losses of the previous month.

Stalin had called Tolbuchin personally from the Kremlin to congratulate him and there had been an official cable from the *Stavka*[1]. The new puppet Communist government, picked long before in Moscow, had made a brief appearance, fighting their way to HQ through the long stream of their fellow citizens being herded eastwards by the NKVD, armed with whips, to 'thank our Soviet brothers for the boon of freedom now conferred upon us'.

Now the Russians were alone, celebrating their victory in the typical Russian fashion by getting blind drunk, as if that were the only way to escape from the grim reality of their daily lives. But Tolbuchin, renowned throughout the Army for his drinking ability, had no stomach for the celebration. Despondently he sipped his pepper vodka and waited for news of the missing train.

That damned priest had turned the tables on him. What if it came out that he had taken a bribe? He took a hasty sip at his vodka and shuddered slightly at the thought. Everyone in the top echelons knew just how corrupt Stalin and the rest of his cronies

---

1. Soviet High Command

of the Kremlin's inner circle were, with their women, the orgies, their accumulation of treasure; all the same 'Old Leather Face' tried to maintain the appearance of simple peasant morality to the outer world. He would not hesitate one minute to punish even a Marshal of the Soviet Union if he thought he had been bribed.

The telephone on the desk in front of him rang. No one else noticed it save a gloomy, sober Suslov. Tolbuchin picked up the phone and barked 'Speak!' Suslov watched the Commander of the Ukrainian Front curiously, wondering what was so important about the telephone call.

Tolbuchin eventually put down the receiver and stared blankly into space for a while. Abruptly he became aware of Suslov's scrutiny. He flushed almost angrily and then his red-faced, angry look was changed to one of thoughtfulness. He crooked a big finger at the Major.

Suslov rose immediately and shoving his way through the drunken staff officers came to attention in front of the Army Commander. 'Comrade Commander!'

'Suslov, I regret that I was not in a position to allow your Grey Eagles to take part in the final assault on the position of those SS swine. It didn't fit into my plans, although I know you requested that honour as revenge for what they did to your battalion in the Vétes Mountains.'

Tolbuchin looked up at him cunningly. 'What would you say if I told you that all those Fritz SS men did not perish on the Castle Hill?'

Suslov looked at him sharply. 'What?'

'Yes, that phone call just reported that one of our partisan units has brushed with a train-load of Hungarian civilians – capitalist trash the lot of them – fleeing westwards to their German allies. During the course of the fighting they noted SS men among the defenders. The sole German casualty bore the armband of the *Europa*. Now what do you say to that, Suslov?'

'What are we doing about. it, Comrade Marshal?' Suslov asked, trying to control his excitement.

'Under the present circumstances and weather conditions in the mountains, very little until they reach our frontline.' He paused slightly.

Suslov rose to the bait. 'Comrade Marshal,' he said, 'in the name of my dead Eagles and their living comrades, I request permission to deal with those Fritz SS. They owe my Eagles a debt – in blood.'

Tolbuchin's brain was racing. Suslov was a very violent and a very loyal man. In his present frame of mind, neither the Germans nor the Hungarians would ever survive if he and his Eagles caught up with them. They would wipe them out in revenge for the Vértes Mountains business. But he had to make quite sure that Suslov would keep his mouth shut later, come what may.

'You realize the difficulties, the weather, the terrain, the fact that the Fritzes have somehow or other stolen a small armoured train?'

'I know no difficulties, Comrade Marshal. I see only murdered Eagles, who demand their revenge from the other side of the grave.'

'How would you do it?' Tolbuchin inquired, still not revealing his hand. 'The terrain is so snowbound now that none of our own armour in the area could ever get through in time. And infantry wouldn't have a hope in hell against an armoured train.'

Suslov seized eagerly at the chance offered him. 'Paradrop – somewhere twenty or thirty kilometres ahead of the train in a spot where I would have time to prepare a defence – perhaps destroy the track, that sort of thing, Comrade Marshal.'

'*Paradrop!*' Tolbuchin exclaimed. 'You must be mad, Suslov – in this weather!'

'Comrade Marshal,' Suslov said proudly, his eyes gleaming. 'Every last one of my Eagles is prepared to lay down his life to pay back the debt in blood.' Tolbuchin knew he had the fool. The man was too good to be true. 'All right, Suslov,' he said slowly, 'I shall let you and your Eagles go – but you go without permission. If anyone finds out, I know nothing. You understand that?' he added severely.

'I do.'

'Good. Let me give you this piece of advice to avoid future complications. When you ambush that train make sure that not a single Fritz or Hungarian civilian remains alive.' He looked hard at the other man. 'Is that clear?' Suslov's face was expressionless, but when he spoke, his words were eloquent testimony of just how ruthless he would be.

'Clear, Comrade Marshal. Not one of them, soldier, civilian, man, woman or child will survive. My Eagles will see to that.'

THREE

The train was deep in the spectacular mountain country, which bordered Lake Balaton. The snow blizzard had passed and from where Schulze sat, he could see the rails, glittering in the winter sun, as they wound round and round the mountainside, through the white firs, until they reached the spidery, gleaming metal bridge spanning the gorge ahead. Everything was bright, sparkling, seen with the preternatural clarity of vision that always follows a fall of snow.

'Sergeant-Major Schulze, could I have your attention?'

Schulze took his eyes from the view. The old Jew was speaking. 'On the other side of that bridge, Schulze, there is a very steep descent almost to the valley floor along which the main Russian line runs. Now, if my information is correct, the Russians have barricaded the line there. They have not destroyed it because they hope to use it to transport their own troops westwards once their advance starts again. Nor have your own people on the other side of the valley destroyed their section of the line. Presumably they have the same hope of using it if they resume the offensive again. Look!' He shoved the map across the table towards Schulze.

The descent looked very steep indeed to judge from the contours, with the track swinging round a bend and going straight down to the valley floor. He used his thumb to measure the length of the straight run against the distance scale. It was about a third of a kilometre.

Well?' Janosz asked finally.

'Well, what?'

'Have you any suggestions on how to get through that barrier? According to my informant it is composed of old track and wooden sleepers from the permanent way, reinforced with drums of concrete.'

'We could ram it,' Schulze said thoughtfully, stroking his big unshaven chin. 'This train carries some weight.'

'But we could well derail the train and block the line by doing so,' Janosz objected.

'Yes, you're right there.' He thought for a few moments. 'What about using one of the coaches as a battering ram?'

Janosz considered the suggestion for a moment or two, then shook his head. 'No good, Schulze. Firstly you can see how packed we all are in here. We need that coach. Secondly, an armoured coach like that would make all further progress impossible if it crashed into the barrier and remained across the lines. Our locomotive would not have the power to remove it and pull the rest of the train at the same time.'

Schulze grunted his agreement and for a few minutes the planners sank into a gloomy silence, as the heavy train chugged closer and closer to the bridge. But in the end it was neither of them who came up with the answer. It was Chink.

Shuddering and turning his green face away hastily from the window as he spotted yet another sheer slope falling hundreds of metres to the valley, he said: 'Chink think van.'

'*Chink think van,*' Schulze mimicked him. 'What the hell is that supposed to mean?'

'Van, he break up when hit barrier. Van, he can be steered. Van, he – '

Janosz held up his skinny hand for silence. 'Of course!' he exclaimed. 'The van has its own steering, enough to keep it on the track at high speed.'

'And it's not as heavy as the coaches,' Schulze agreed eagerly. 'Now if I could get my boys in position on either side of that slope without the Popovs spotting them down below, we could steer the van into that barricade and in the confusion, my boys could fix the Popovs' hash for them. Then Attila could bring the train down and we'd be off towards the German lines.'

'But who go drive van?' the Chink asked in all innocence.

Schulze beamed at him wickedly. Who you think go drive van? Chink and me!'

The Jewish refugees worked with a will clearing the deep frozen snow from the loop line at the top of the height. Behind them, Attila was defreezing the locked switch from the main to the branch line with a blow torch, while his fireman, shovelling mightily, was keeping up the steam pressure, knowing that at this height it could not be allowed to fall.

Schulze himself was busy with his handful of young men. He had divided them into two groups. Now clad in white silk sheets as snow camouflage, they waited expectantly. Schulze glanced hastily at his watch. 'You've got about fifteen minutes. I want you around the bend and in position on both sides of the track by then. Once the van is within a couple of hundred metres of the barricade, you go in – hard.'

Moments later the men had disappeared round the bend and were advancing cautiously on the Soviet positions far below. The working party had cleared the snow and the points were free. The train could move in. Schulze grinned at Janosz, leaning broken-lunged on his shovel. 'Harder than sitting in your parlour counting your money, ain't it, Yid?'

Now things moved swiftly. Attila drove the train into the loop and uncoupled the engine. He backed down the track and came up at the rear of the little guards van. Swiftly he and his fireman uncoupled it from the train, coupled it up to his engine and drew it out of the loop on to the main line. With a clatter of driving wheels on the steep icy rails, Attila pushed the van almost to the top of the slope. There he and the fireman again uncoupled the van. 'I'll shunt you beyond the height just where the slow curve begins, After that you're on your own. The best of luck.' He said the final words as if they were the last he would ever address to the two SS men.

Schulze dismissed him, very businesslike now. 'All right, Chink, you stand by the door all the time, savvy?' Chink, his face green already, could not answer. He nodded his head fearfully. 'It's your job to see that it stays wide open, whatever happens. When I give the word you jump. Because if you don't, I'm going to give you a big kick up your yellow ass, which will send you out all right – then I'm coming after you.'

Behind them the locomotive's wheels clattered on the slope and it began to take the strain. Slowly they edged their way towards the bend. Schulze gulped and seized the brass handle of the steering wheel to the rear of the van. This was it!

The van rolled forward very slowly. Not more than ten kilometres an hour, Schulze judged. The rockwall of the bend loomed ever larger. To their right, the mountain fell away in a sheer drop. Schulze tightened his grip on the brass handled wheel.

And then they were around the bend. Far below Schulze caught a glimpse of a few dark houses and some tiny figures plodding stolidly through the deep snow. The barrier guards. He concentrated his attention on the van which was gathering speed. Schulze licked suddenly dry lips and felt the wheel shiver violently in his sweating grip. He held on desperately, fighting with all his great strength to keep the van on the track.

Now the countryside was hissing past in a crazy white and green blur. Schulze leaned forward and with all his strength applied the brake. Blue angry sparks flew from the wheels – so high that he could see them flashing by the open door. Nothing happened! He stared at the wild blur outside in horror. He had to slow the thing before the barrier so that they could jump to safety!

'STOP, YOU BASTARD!' Schulze screamed and thudded his shoulder against the brake with the last of his strength. The screech of the locked wheels reached a terrifying pitch. It seemed as if death itself was rushing remorselessly towards them. Then when it appeared the van would never brake, the terrible bedlam of screeching metal diminished. The blur steadied to a series of identifiable objects. Schulze waited no longer. He raised his big boot and planted a tremendous kick in Chink's baggy pants. He screamed and went sailing out into the snow.

Schulze raised his boot once more and smashed it against the brake. As the van started to accelerate again, he dived full length through the door. He landed heavily in the deep snow, all breath knocked from his body. Below little, white-clad figures were running clumsily through the heavy snow on both sides of the track towards the dark barricade. They were his men and the surprised Russians had still not reacted, though they were now doubling towards their positions.

Just as the first of them swung themselves behind the machine-guns, tearing them round to face the attackers, the van smashed full tilt into the barricade. There was the great echoing sound of metal striking metal, followed an instant later by the detonation of the High Explosives with which Schulze had packed the front of the van as an afterthought. Next moment the barricade turned to a mass of flying debris, thick black smoke, and falling bodies. Schulze raised himself and started to look for Chink. The path was open again.

FOUR

The armoured train rolled to a stop in the shattered little station. Behind it, the Russian fire which had pursued the train through no-man's land started to peter out. Cautiously the infantry of a second-class *Luftwaffe* field division guarding that part of the line raised their heads from their positions in the ruins to stare at the train. It was decorated with the crossed flags of Germany and Hungary on the front of the locomotive, and both sides of the leading coach bore a large swastika.

The elderly Captain, a comb-out from the *Luftwaffe* Ministry, Berlin, watched as the door of the leading coach opened. Two young SS troopers – he could tell they were SS from their camouflaged overalls – sprang out smartly and took up their positions, machine-pistols at the alert. They were followed by another who unrolled – of all things – a strip of red carpet. A fourth appeared. A giant of a man, an NCO obviously, his barrel chest covered with decorations. He took up his position facing the door, waiting expectantly.

The Captain made a decision. The train was all right, and judging from the SS men, it contained someone of importance. He thrust his pistol into its holster and snapped: 'All right on your feet and follow me.' Reluctantly his collection of frightened old men and boys obeyed his command.

On the platform, the three SS men had crashed their boots down on the battle-littered concrete and sprung rigidly to attention, as if the Führer himself were going to make an appearance at any moment.

The figure who emerged was small and old and very wrinkled, with a dark, hook-nosed face that the captain took to be Hungarian. He was dressed in a light blue uniform, his skinny chest almost covered in decorations, on both sides of the tunic. For no apparent reason as he stepped on to the red carpet, he touched his hand to his high, shiny-peaked cap, with that casual manner of saluting which always, in the Captain's experience, indicated a very high-ranking officer.

'*Heil Hitler!*' the three SS men bellowed in unison, as if they were on guard outside the Berlin Reich Chancellory and Hitler himself had just appeared. '*Heil Hitler, Herr Generalfeldmarschall!*'

'Field-Marshal!' Captain Blomberg of the 4th *Luftwaffe* Field Division could hardly believe his ears. A Field-Marshal in his section of the front. In the last four weeks, the highest ranking visitor he had received in this remote part of rural Hungary had been the divisional surgeon making inquiries about his company's VD incidence. He started to walk towards the train, from which a group of civilians were now beginning to descend.

The big SS NCO heard the sound of his boots. He swung round and viewed the scruffy old company of *Luftwaffe* soldiers coming out of the ruins, weapons now slung over their bent shoulders. 'Officer in charge?' he bellowed.

'Here,' Blomberg heard himself saying, like a schoolboy reporting at the morning roll-call. 'Here Sergeant-Major.' He felt himself flushing even as he said the words. 'Blomberg is my name – Captain Blomberg.'

'Over here, *Captain* Blomberg,' the big NCO barked. Blomberg marched forward and clicking his heels together in his best imitation of the elegant staff officers at the Ministry, he saluted.

The Field-Marshal acknowledged his salute. 'Report?' he said in excellent German.

'*Captain Blomberg, Commander of 8th Company, 1st Regiment, Fourth Luftwaffe Field Division.* Four men sick, one man wounded, one hundred and thirty effectives, Field-Marshal,' he barked, looking at some distant object behind the skinny Hungarian's right shoulder in the approved fashion.

'Thank you, Captain Blomberg,' the Field-Marshal said and held out his wrinkled hand graciously. 'My name is Jerzcy von Stuhlweissenburg. I am responsible for bringing out the last Hungarian cabinet.' He extended a hand towards the under sized, middle-aged, somewhat shabbily dressed civilians standing a little uneasily behind him on the platform. Captain Blomberg was overwhelmed. 'But how. . . what . . . why?' He seemed unable to get the questions out.

'We have escaped from Budapest at the risk of our lives and with the help of your brave SS soldiers.' He indicated the massive NCO, who towered above the civilians and the shabby *Luftwaffe* soldiers. 'Now we are tired. We need rest and food – and help.' With a spontaneous gesture, he unpinned one of the myriad decorations on his skinny chest, pinned it on Captain Blomberg's unadorned tunic. 'The Star of St Stefan, First class, Captain,' he announced. 'It is yours in anticipation of the help you will give us.'

'Anything that is within my power, Herr Generalfeldmarschall,' Blomberg snapped, already feeling several centimetres taller.

'Good,' the Field Marshal said graciously. 'Let us get my people under cover. We shall of course need hot food. Then I shall want you to telephone all along the route we will be taking to Berchtesgaden – '

'Oh, my God,' Blomberg said to himself, 'they're on their way to see the Führer.'

'And ensure that we have no difficulties with petty officialdom. We have wasted enough time as it is – and time is of the essence, is it not, Captain?'

'Of course, Field-Marshal,' Blomberg agreed hastily. 'But please follow me, if you would be so kind.'

As he swept past the SS men, who were standing rigidly to attention, the Field-Marshal winked solemnly at Sergeant-Major

Schulze, whose face was full of admiration. They had pulled it off. They were through the German line.

That long afternoon, while the *Luftwaffe* men, harassed by an anxious Blomberg, prepared a gigantic pea-soup, Schulze and Janosz prepared the rest of their route into Austria.

'From Mencsel' Janosz explained, 'the direct route leads to Vienna. But that is too dangerous. There are too many unpleasant questions that could be asked and we don't want that, do we?'

Schulze agreed. The closer they came to the Reich, the more he was becoming aware of the danger. These desperate days, the authorities were quick to act once the 'head-hunters' of the military police picked up a deserter: it was against a wall and a quick burst of machine-gun fire. Courts-martial were looked on as a waste of time.

'That uniformed fool will fix up our route to Berchtesgaden via Vienna. Once he has done that we shall switch direction at Bratislava. From there we will bear south-west and enter Austria in the *Burgenland* area – here. It is a country of little villages, few towns and a poor populace, who are not immune – '

'To Christian charity,' Schulze beat him to it.

'Yes, money will make our way easier,' Janosz agreed. 'Now, I intend that we move on to the secondary line – here – and cross the Austrian frontier at the small village of Pamhagen. If we are lucky, we shall only have to contend with the single frontier guard who is also the local gendarme and undertaker.'

Schulze could guess that Janosz had been engaged in this business of smuggling people – Jews most likely – across frontiers for a long time now. In 1938 and 1939 there had probably been many Austrian and German Jews he had helped across that lonely frontier.

'What about us after that?' he asked instead.

'You could go with us the whole way.'

'To Palestine?' Schulze cried.

'You are a useful man. We of the *Hagannah* will have need of you in the days to come.'

'What and have my dick shortened like a Yid? No thank you, Janosz.' He paused. 'But it's a long way back to Hamburg and the head hunters are everywhere in Germany today.'

'I shall help you, if that is your wish.'

'You mean you've got some of these *Hagannah* Yids of yours in Germany, too?' Schulze asked incredulously.

'Yes. We have. We are everywhere.' He smiled slightly. 'Once the people have eaten and the train has been refuelled, we shall leave. I don't want to spend a night so close to the frontline. One never knows when the Russians might attack.'

Schulze rose and slung his machine-pistol. 'All right, Field-Marshal, let's go and see if the Hungarian cabinet have finished stuffing their guts with pea soup and sausage yet.'

FIVE

The jump in the blinding snowstorm had been a catastrophe. Suslov had warned his Grey Eagles of the danger in advance, but not one of them had backed down. Revenge for their murdered comrades overrode all other considerations. At ground level the wind velocity had been forecast as seven metres per second. Instead it turned out to be twice that speed. The casualties had been appalling. Man after man had had his chute caught by the howling wind, fought desperately to empty the air out of it, and been borne away across the white waste never to be seen again.

By dawn Suslov had collected exactly one hundred survivors and of that pathetic handful of men some twelve were seriously injured and had to be left behind – at their own request. But that was not all. As soon as the snow had ceased to fall and he had been able to orientate himself, he had found that instead of being well inside the Soviet lines in Hungary, he was twenty kilometres behind the German front!

The Grey Eagles had been cut off behind the Fritzes' line often enough in the past. What concerned Suslov more was that he no longer knew which direction the runaway train was taking inside the German front.

Fortunately the sole surviving radio operator had managed to pick up Tolbuchin's message that 'object X' (as he put it so carefully) had broken through the Soviet front at Mencsel. Suslov did some quick map work. There was no branch line leading off either north or south from the track which ran westwards from Mencsel to Bratislava. The line did not divide until the Austrian border where branches were needed to deploy as many troops as possible quickly along the frontier.

It seemed that he could be sure that the missing train was continuing in the direction of Bratislava. He must stop them somewhere along that line. But where? The train's speed would have to be greatly reduced. It had to be somewhere where he could spring an ambush. After all, his men were armed with nothing heavier than automatic pistols.

One hour after receiving Tolbuchin's message, he found the ideal spot. It was some thirty kilometres to the east of Bratislava. A small hamlet, at the foot of a very steep ascent, where, according to his detailed military map, there was a watering and fuelling stop as required by any train approaching the height. His mind made up, he had ordered a speed march to the little, lonely railway hamlet. His men had performed splendidly, covering the twelve kilometres in two hours, despite the snow. The place had been just what he wanted. The railway track ran through a steep gully beyond the collection of wooden cottages and tiny station which made up the hamlet and then began to climb rapidly. On one side the track was bordered by an almost vertical cliff; on the other, the shallow slope was strewn with snow-covered rocks, deposited there in the previous century by the engineers who had blasted a passage through the mountain. They would make ideal cover for the bulk of his force.

The Eagles had killed the handful of inhabitants as a matter of routine; they could not afford any betrayal so far behind the enemy lines. The only man Suslov spared was the ancient, ashen-faced station-master. Suslov needed him to stop the armoured train.

His plan was complete. Up among the rocks above the hamlet, be had sixty men in position, with the remainder hidden about the rickety wooden station, ready and alert. Satisfied he turned to Schmitt, a Volga German, and said idly: 'Ask him what they call this place?' He jerked a careless thumb at the trembling station-master.

Schmitt put the question into German. For a minute the station-master was unable to answer. He opened his mouth, his white lips trembled, but nothing came out but meaningless grunts.

'Punch him!' Suslov ordered. 'But not too hard.' Schmitt punched him in the stomach and then slapped him across the face for good measure, before putting his question again.

The old man quavered something or other.

Well?' Suslov demanded, not taking his eyes off the line.

'Dodemann Pass,' Schmitt answered. 'That's its name in the local dialect.'

'And what does that mean in Russian?'

'Dead Man's Pass, Comrade Commander.'

Suslov smiled icily. 'An appropriate name,' he commented, 'a very appropriate name – for them!'

The armoured train was slowing down now to conserve fuel. Attila knew that once they did not show up in Bratislava, the station authorities would start making inquiries; they would have to go all out then along the branch line to get to Pamhagen. Perhaps, the surly driver considered, he should make a fuelling stop at Dodemann Station. In the leading coach, most of the tired civilians and SS troopers sprawled on the gangway floor were snoring gently, believing now that they were out of real danger.

Schulze and Chink, who had kicked a couple of the younger Jews out of their seats on to the floor in order to sit in comfort, discussed their own plans softly, while the others slept.

They stopped short, suddenly all tiredness and the projected acquisition of a *Reeperbahn* brothel gone from their minds. The train was slowly coming to a halt, although no stop was scheduled until the Austrian border. Schulze sprang to his feet and simultaneously blew his whistle and kicked a snoring SS man in the ribs to waken him.

In an instant all was noisy confusion as the middle-aged civilians and the soldiers started from their sleep, the civilians fearfully,
the soldiers solely concerned with grabbing their weapons and
getting to their posts in the armoured train before it came to a
final halt.

Attila swore viciously. The station-master was standing in the
middle of the track, opposite the empty platform, waving his
red-and-white tin *kelle*[1], as if he were at Budapest's main station
instead of this provincial dump. He could either run the silly old
fool down, or stop. He decided to stop. Perhaps he could coal
up here after all.

He began to ease the brake back and close the throttle. The
driving wheels locked, there was a soft clatter of buffers and
the armoured train finally came to a halt just as Sergeant-Major
Schulze dropped into the cab with an urgent: 'Why are we stop-
ping?'

Attila took his hand off the throttle. 'Him,' he said laconically.
Schulze peered over the side towards the old man, dressed in a
shabby uniform. 'The old boy looks as if he's going to wet his
knickers at any moment,' he commented.

Schulze felt there could be nothing to fear this far behind the
German front. Besides, apart from the old Hungarian, the place
appeared deserted.

'I'll see if he's got any coal in his bunker for us,' Attila said.
'Yes, the old *Monsignor*'ll give him some of his famous Christian
charity if he comes across with some.'

'You have any coal?' Attila the Hun cried, leaning out of his cab.
'We'll see there's something –' He never finished the sentence.

Firing from the open station window, Suslov, who had had his
automatic pistol trained on the cab these last sixty seconds, caught
the Hungarian driver with a full burst. Attila screamed, his face

---

1. A signalling device used on continental railways instead of a flag or
   whistle.

suddenly ripped apart and jetting blood. He was dead before he reached the snow-covered earth.

'Down!' Schulze screamed, just as the little hamlet erupted with angry small arms fire. As he hit the cinder-covered metal floor, he knew, with a hopeless sinking feeling, that they had walked right into a trap.

SIX

Schulze sagged against the inside of the door. 'Shit!' he breathed and mopped his sweat-lathered brow in relief. 'I thought the bastards had done for me back there.'

Janosz, unafraid but clearly very worried, tugged a small bottle out of his pocket and thrust it towards the bareheaded NCO. 'Here, drink some of my medicine,' he cried above the vicious snap and crackle of the battle outside. Schulze seized the bottle gratefully. He downed its contents and coughed throatily.

'It's bad out there. The engine driver's copped it. They're dug in in strength on both sides of the rail and there's a lot more of the Ivan buggers further up the slope. I've got the Swede on the cab with the fireman – he's got the other spandau and we've taken no casualties, except for a couple of flesh wounds from ricochets.'

'The fireman – can he drive the engine?' Janosz demanded. 'Yes, I think so. But at the moment, he's scared shitless – there's not much we can do with him. He's certainly not going to move the train forward.'

'*Forward*, you say,' Janosz emphasized the word, a sudden flash of hope in his dark eyes. 'What do you think they'll do?'

'They can't hang around here for ever, so far behind our lines. My guess is they can do one of two things: they'll ask us to surrender or they'll rush us as soon as it is dark enough to do so. In both cases they'll attempt to collar the train for themselves so that they can barrel their way through those hopeless *Luftwaffe* sods back there into their own positions.'

'And if we surrender?'

Schulze made a gesture with his big forefinger, as if he were pulling a trigger.

'But why?' Janosz protested. 'We haven't injured them in any way. Why are we so important?'

Schulze shrugged. 'Better ask Stalin that. But if they think we're important enough to send troops in so far behind enemy lines, you can bet your last *matzo*, they're not going to just shake our hands and tell us to go home – the game's over. No, if we surrender, we're for the chop!'

'Do you really think so?' Janosz said horrified 'I don't really think so – I know so.'

'*Ceasefire!*' Suslov yelled, hands cupped around his mouth.

'Stop firing everywhere – there's no need to waste any further ammunition!' Across the way in the trapped armoured train, the firing ceased too, as if in anticipation of the ambushers' next move.

The echoing silence which followed was broken by the voice of Schmitt, the Volga German, speaking the dialect that his German forefathers had brought to Russia nearly three centuries before It was strange yet comprehensible, as it boomed through the megaphone: 'Germans, you have one chance – surrender!'

'Fuck off!' Schulze yelled.

'Come out with your weapons,' Schmitt went on. 'Throw them to the ground immediately you leave the train and then raise your hands. Continue walking to the station-house. You will not be harmed. All we want is the train. You can go on your own way. We will not harm you,' the metallic voice echoed and re-echoed across the battle-littered snow. 'Surrender now!' Schmitt lowered the megaphone and waited.

There was no reaction from the train.

'Fritz bastards,' Suslov cursed. He knew that time was running out for the Eagles too. In spite of the fact that they had cut the wires connecting the remote hamlet with the outside world, it was after all on the main line to Bratislava. Someone would discover them on the German side sooner or later. He glanced at the afternoon sky. It was darkening rapidly. The snow would begin to fall again soon.

He jabbed his elbow angrily into the Volga German's side. 'Try them again!' he ordered.

'All right, Gypsy, are you ready?' Schulze asked, crouching next to him in the armoured cab.

'Will they fire?' the fireman quavered.

'Well, they won't exactly be throwing roses at us,' Schulze snorted. 'You ready too, Swede?' The dour blonde Swedish SS man, manning the machine-gun on the tender grunted a moody 'yes'.

'All right,' Schulze commanded. 'NOW!'

The fireman let go of the brake and opened the throttle wide. For one brief moment, the driving wheels spun on the icy rails and the clouds of dark smoke belched from the stack purposelessly. Then the wheels bit. The armoured train began to roll.

'The Fritzes are moving, Comrade Commander!' Schmitt cried. Suslov sat up and peered through the shattered window. 'Fire!' he yelled angrily. '*Fire – Eagles!*'

'But they're moving, Comrade Commander!' Schmitt protested. Instead of moving up the slope ahead, the train was rapidly puffing back down the way it had come, the Eagles' fire wildly off mark.

'Ceasefire…ceasefire.' He rose to his feet and shouted the command, knowing that his men were wasting their ammunition. The train was already almost behind the cover of the next bend.

'What will they do now, Comrade Commander?' Schmitt asked. 'Our patrols have torn up the track a kilometre from here. That's as far as they will be able to get.'

'What will they do?' Suslov echoed his question. 'Once they know that there is no way back, they will attempt to rush the slope with their train – even if they abandoned the train, there is no road, no other way up over the mountain save that railway pass. And when they make that attempt we will have a little surprise waiting for them, Schmitt – a very unpleasant little surprise.'

'*Here they come again, Comrade Commander!*' Schmitt shouted. Suslov awoke immediately from an uneasy doze. He sprang to his feet, machine-pistol at the alert. The armoured train was steaming round the bend at top speed, a menacing black outlined against the streaming white of the snowstorm. Suslov fired a quick burst into the air to alert the men in the station and higher up on the slope. 'Stand by!' he barked and dropped behind his cover once again.

Ragged firing broke out on all sides. Suslov could hear the slugs whining off the train's metal sides. He took careful aim as the locomotive, great clouds of brown smoke steaming from its stack, came ever closer. He fired, but the tracer bounced off the cab's armour like hailstones. With a great clatter of wheels and hiss of escaping steam, the train hurtled through the station, not one shot coming from it.

The black locomotive smashed through the barrier they had erected across the line, tossing the sleepers high into the air, as if they were made of matchwood. It rattled on, its speed obviously diminishing now, as it started to take the steep slope. Suslov cried to his men to follow him and they ran heavily through the streaming snow towards their comrades dug in higher up.

The train, its speed considerably slower now, laboured up the steep slope ever closer to the Eagles' positions. Thick smoke streamed from its stack and the waiting men, tensed over their weapons, could hear the strain the locomotive was undergoing.

It was almost alongside them now. Behind the rocks, the Eagles tensed. The senior NCO raised his hand and then brought it down sharply as the locomotive came level with is hiding place. A line of violet flashes ran the length of the Eagles' positions.

Tracer flew through the snow like a swarm of angry red and white hornets and slugs whined off the armour. Yet still there was no answering fire from the train. It might have well been some ghost train, steaming through the dark, eerily impervious to human influence. Now the Eagles were standing up everywhere, unafraid and confident that the men within were condemned already. Their faces, wet with melting snow, were wild like those of country boys at some local fair blazing away at a shooting booth. Still the train did not falter in its course.

It passed through the last Russian position and began the final stage of the ascent, the Eagles' fire dying away behind it.

All noise, save that of the locomotive labouring its way upwards, ceased as the Russians shouldered their weapons and watched it go to its death.

Crump! The crash of the first explosion, accompanied by a blinding white flash, merged almost simultaneously with the second. For a moment nothing seemed to happen, and Suslov thought with a flash of horror that his trap had failed. Then the train came to an abrupt halt and the two rear coaches toppled sideways, hesitating as if they were fighting to avoid the terrible fate awaiting them. Next instant they sailed out into the void of the precipice. Almost lazily they turned over in mid-air, while the Eagles watched, their mouths open in awe, and then with ever increasing speed they tumbled to the valley floor below. With a thunderclap of sound, they crashed to the bottom.

The locomotive and the first coach still teetered on the edge of the line. Steam was escaping furiously from the locomotive's ruptured boiler. Then the first coach began to sway, until it could be held by the shattered locomotive no longer. Amid the rending of metal and the splintering of heavy sleepers, the great black monster was dragged inexorably over the edge of the precipice. A second later it hit the valley floor and exploded with a great echoing roar that seemed to go on forever.

SEVEN

'Well?' Suslov demanded.

The snow-covered Eagle hauled himself over the edge of rock and slumped down in the snow, his big chest heaving with the effort of the long climb.

'What did you find?' Suslov asked again, impatient to hear just how successful their operation had been so that they could begin making their way back to their own lines under the cover of the snowstorm. The Eagle swallowed hard and looked up at his C.O., his face crimson and wet with melting snow. 'Nothing, Comrade Commander,' he answered.

'What ?' Suslov's voice expressed utter bafflement – a shattering of comprehension.

The climber pulled himself to his feet. 'I said, Comrade Commander, that the coaches were empty. There wasn't a soul in either of the two I managed to reach.'

'But that's…that's impossible,' Suslov stuttered, his legendary calm destroyed for the first time in many years of war. 'It can't be!'

The climber shrugged, an air of injured patience on his broad White Russian face. 'Then I suggest you go down there and have a look yourself, Comrade Commander.'

Suslov was too shaken to notice the impertinence. 'Did you check the locomotive?' he snapped quickly.

'Yes.'

'And what did you find?'

But the broad-shouldered climber never answered that question. For at that moment, Sven Hassel, the Swede, his lean face set in a look of implacable cruelty, squeezed the trigger of his spandau and sent a high-pitched burst of bullets into the group around the climber. The stream of lead ripped into his broad chest and he sailed over the edge of the precipice, trailing a long, thin scream after him.

The burst of machine-gun fire from the height overlooking the Eagles' positions was the signal the little force of SS men had been waiting for. Machine-guns burst in frenetic, frightening life.

'*Down!*' Suslov screamed desperately. But it was already too late. The attack caught them completely in the open. Man after man went down, some screaming, some silent, some with a violent, threshing of their arms, some gently as if they were eager to lie down on the soft carpet of snow and die. It was a massacre!

'Every man for himself!' Suslov cried desperately, knowing that his Eagles were finished. Now it was a question of saving one's skin. Everywhere his Eagles dropped their weapons and tried to run for it. It was futile. They fell on all sides, mown down by the murderous weight of fire.

Suslov was consumed by a burning, overwhelming hatred which triumphed over all fear. If he had to die, then he would make the Fritz bastards pay the price for his death. Raising his head as much as he dared, feeling the cold wind of the bullets scything through the air only millimetres above it, he surveyed the scene. There were machine-guns on the three heights to their north, south and east. The sheer side of the precipice was not covered though. Why should it be? The Fritzes obviously thought no-one could get out that way. No-one but Major Suslov, Commander of the Grey Eagles.

Suddenly he was up on his feet and running, bounding nimbly over the bodies of his dead soldiers, pushing those still not dead out of his way, running straight for the cliff-edge. The

Fritzes spotted him almost instantly. Lead struck the ground all around him. He zig-zagged crazily. Time and time again the bullets missed. Then he was hit. A burning, searing pain in his right thigh. For a moment he felt he must fall. Abruptly the pain had gone and in that same instant he was diving over the edge of the cliff and out of sight.

Schulze took off his helmet and waved it over his head wildly. 'That's it,' he cried, jubilation in his voice that the plan had succeeded. They had a long walk in front of them to Austria, but now the way was clear at last. 'Stop your firing. Knock it off there.' Reluctantly the young SS troopers took their fingers off their triggers, as if they could not get enough of death, eyes gleaming with an almost sexual excitement.

Janosz left the gun he had been manning and started to limp over to Schulze. The killing had finished and he was glad. There had been too much killing in Europe, a whole half a decade of it. He wanted to see no more of it. Palestine would mean peace.

He halted in front of Schulze, who was surveying the dead Russians lying everywhere in the snow in front of them 'I shall go and fetch my people now.'

Schulze nodded and turned to Chink. 'You'd better go with him and give him some cover.'

'Right-o, Schulzi,' said Chink, who had suggested the way of jamming the locomotive's throttle which had formed the basis of their plan. Now the Jews were without a train, but Schulze could imagine that Janosz's cunning mind and a liberal use of 'Christian charity' would find some other way of getting his refugees to Italy. There was no doubt about that

'And make it snappy,' Schulze ordered. 'We want to be over the border by morning.'

'I make Yid move like very hell,' Chink said happily, slinging his rifle. 'Schulzi and Chink must get Hamburg, open knocking-shop –'

A face suddenly appeared over the edge of the cliff-side. A terrible face, torn, lacerated, flayed into a mass of red gore by the rocks, out of which blazed two absolutely wild, animal eyes, filled, with unspeakable hatred. A clawlike hand, from which the flesh trailed in dripping red strips, rose into the air. Chink saw the black round object it held. 'No!' he screamed and held up his hands, as if to ward it off with his naked flesh.

But it was hopeless. The grenade sailed through the air and exploded at his feet. It caught Chink in its blazing, whirling fury, threw him high into the air, and when his terribly mutilated body smashed to the ground again, something rolled a few paces away to come to rest at Schulze feet in the snow. It was Chink's head.

Schulze screamed. In a bound he had grabbed the dying Suslov and dragged him over the edge of the cliff. His face contorted by a bestial fury, he brought down his heavy boot, studded with thirteen hobnails, and crashed it into Suslov's face. Time and time again. Bone splintered. Blood spurted out in scarlet jets from nose, ears, eyes. The eyes disappeared. Still Schulze did not stop. On and on he went, the only sound that of his own savage grunting breath, the moans from the man who was being stamped into the ground, and that persistent crunch-crunch of heavy metal against soft flesh.

Janosz could not bear to look. He had never seen such unspeakable ferocity in a human face in all his long life. It belonged to another world.

And finally Schulze was done. Sergeant-Major Schulze, the last survivor of *SS Regiment Wotan*, sank into the snow beside the man he had just killed, the tears streaming down his suddenly transformed, sweat-lathered face. '*This fucking war,*' he sobbed. '*This fucking, awful war.*'

ENVOI

ENVOI

Schulze had been drunk for the whole week they had been waiting in Graz. One by one or in small groups, he had seen his little band of SS troopers, clad in the civilian clothes Janosz had bought them on the black market, depart. Now they were all on their way to face the brutal uncertainties of their own countries in which they would be regarded as renegades and traitors and not the bold 'defenders of Western European culture against the red Bolshevik plague', as the black and red SS recruiting posters had once screamed. Some of them were going to their death, some to long terms of imprisonment; but those of them who survived the bitter years ahead would carry to the grave the terrible stigma of being Europe's lost sons – ex-members of *SS Regiment Europa*.

Now Janosz himself was ready to leave on the next leg of the long journey to that land of 'milk and honey', as he was calling it openly. With a sizeable portion of that seemingly unlimited 'Christian charity' of his, he had bribed a fat *Wehrmacht* transport Major, who had supplied him with a dozen ancient *Wehrmacht* trucks, complete with ex-Italian POW drivers, glad of this opportunity to return to their own homeland before the Russians came. They would take him and his refugees into Italy and the Allied lines.

Now the time had come for the incongruous pair, the towering, barrel-chested SS NCO and the undersized Jew to part. They stood in the soft-falling snow. Above them, hidden by the grey snow clouds, Soviet bombers were droning westwards on their way to Vienna. They could both hear the rumble of the guns at the front, softening up the German positions for the new offensive. Janosz jerked a thumb in the direction of the artillery barrage.

'They'll be here soon, Schulze,' he said.

Schulze shrugged. 'So what?'

'Europe has got rid of one tyranny,' the little Jew said softly. 'But it will soon be replaced by another one, which will be much worse. I have seen it. Hitler is a novice in cruelty and repression in comparison with Stalin. You will see.'

He held out his hand. 'Well, Schulze, this is the parting of the ways. I must get back to my flock. We move out in thirty minutes, once I get those Italian drivers away from fornicating with the local women.'

'Those Macaronis have got the right idea,' Schulze said, 'fuck not fight.' He took the old man's hand. 'The best of luck, Jew.'

'The same to you, German.' Without another word Janosz turned and walked away, his skinny shoulders bowed against the snowflakes.

Schulze watched him go. He had come a long way with the old Jew – they all had. Now it was all over. For a long moment he stood there on the empty slushy pavement, hearing nothing, seeing nothing, the snow falling sadly on his shabby black-market overcoat, with all his worldly possessions – soap and razor, a handful of useless marks and two hundred Turkish cigarettes – stuffed into its pockets. Ex-Sergeant-Major Schulze felt drained and very, very tired.

Suddenly a soft, winning Austrian voice impinged upon his consciousness, 'Is the gentleman looking for a good time this afternoon?' it inquired.

Schulze spun round, his despair forgotten in an instant. Two teenage girls stood there, dressed in identical peasant costume, their cheeks prettily flushed by the cold air so that a casual observer might well have taken them for country girls. But a delighted

Schulze knew otherwise. Their scarlet lips and the knowing look in their tired eyes told another story. 'You're twins!' he exclaimed somewhat stupidly.

'That's right,' the one who had spoken said, 'you catch on fast.'

'You're going to catch my dick before you're much older, my little cheetah.'

'It'll cost you one hundred *schilling* for a jump,' she replied, unimpressed. 'Which one of us do you fancy?'

'Which *one*?' Schulze roared, tugging out the carton of two hundred cigarettes and noting the sudden look of interest in their jaded eyes. '*Not one, but both of you!*' He thrust the carton at them and putting a big hand around each girl's plump young breasts, he cried out loud, so that the shabby, bent-shouldered civilians on the other side of the street turned in alarm, 'Point me at the nearest bed, my little Austrian darlings! It's going to be the screw of the century, that I can promise you!'

Ex-Sergeant-Major Schulze, the last survivor of that doomed, elite brotherhood, had just declared a separate peace. Now he could begin to live again.